SECRET OF THE ACOLYTES

BESTSELLING AUTHOR

JULIE CALDWELL

1st edition 2025

Paperback ISBN: 979-8-9880180-4-9

Ebook ISBN: 979-8-9880180-5-6

Also by Julie Caldwell

Of Witches and Ruin

Of War and Magic

To everyone who has felt the loss of another

FALL

Chapter One

T HE WROUGHT-IRON GATES TOWERED above me through the sea of dense fog. I looked up at my new home for the next nine months through the slanting rain. The time-worn beige ivy-covered stone of the Gothic-style school seemed to greet me. I sighed silently. Raven's Cove Academy was not the place I wanted to spend the remainder of my high school years. Neither was the small town of Ashton, New Hampshire, but here I was, my mom insisting this was the best boarding school in New England, and that I would fit right in. She was wrong, of course. I didn't want to fit in here. This school was more like a prison sentence than a place to learn. I wanted my old friends, and I wanted my old life.

Mom squeezed my shoulder and grabbed my large suitcase off the sidewalk. She started toward the gate, her slightly damp auburn hair swinging behind her. The hinges swung open with a screech, as if it had been years since anyone had used the entrance. I trudged behind her and jumped when the gate slammed closed.

Inside was warm and dry. The entryway into the main part of the building was enormous, and looked more like the inside of a university or a castle than a high school. A fireplace burned brightly to the left of us in what looked like a grand living room. On the wall hung elegant signs directing us to different areas of the building, and Mom walked toward the one that pointed to the office. I followed as I gaped at the rich, dark wood with wainscoted walls. Black and white pictures hung in ornate gilded frames, and the eyes of the people in them seemed to follow my every move.

A short, older woman, who introduced herself as Ms. Crane, greeted us as we entered the office. Dark hair peppered with gray brushed her shoulders as she shook Mom's hand, then mine. Ms. Crane grabbed a piece of paper off the printer and ushered us upstairs to where I would be staying.

My dorm was on the third floor, and the woman explained that I would share a suite with two other girls, but I would get my own private bedroom.

Small miracles.

I didn't want a roommate to see me cry myself to sleep. My mind flashed back to my last day of freshman year. How had three months passed already? It was too soon to leave home. Too soon to move on...

Three sharp raps brought me back to the present as Ms. Crane knocked on a door that was almost the same dark wood as the walls, but faded with so much use. It lurched open, revealing a well-toned girl with light blond, blown-out hair on the other side.

"Hello Alisa." Ms. Crane motioned me forward. "This is Ophelia Allan. She'll be rooming with you and Bethany. Please make her feel comfortable. Ophelia, this is Alisa Fitzgerald. She will be your Peer Patron."

I waved slightly, and Alisa's returning smile was huge. And very performative.

"What's a Peer Patron?" my mom asked.

Ms. Crane smiled politely and handed Mom the paper, obviously expecting the question.

"Think of it as a den mother, but instead of an older adult, we choose highly qualified upperclassmen that will show the girls the ropes and be there if there's any trouble."

Alisa beamed brighter as she grasped my wrist and led Mom and me inside. The last thing I heard before the door shut was Ms. Crane telling Alisa to make me feel welcome.

Inside the dorm was the same dark-colored wood paneling, but only on the lower half of the walls. The upper half was painted a dark purple, but even with the dark colors, the room didn't feel small at all. There were several tall arched windows that nearly touched the ceiling, their panels coated with the rainfall. Opposite them was a roaring fireplace, the flames flickering with warmth. I had a fireplace inside my dorm? I could get used to that.

Above the mantel hung an immense portrait of a man in a pressed black suit standing and looking every bit as pompous as I imagined someone who had giant paintings of themselves were. Alisa noticed my gaze.

"That's Theodore Kenphrey," she said. "He's the founder of our school. His great-grandson is actually the current headmaster, although they could be twins."

Her tone suggested she was fond of the headmaster, but her eyes held a glimmer of something else. Contempt, maybe. Weird. I brushed it off and angled my head toward her. "He looks...nice...ish."

Alisa giggled, but said nothing, and I turned my attention elsewhere. There were three doors to the left of the fireplace. Alisa guided me and Mom to the one on the right, and my eyes nearly dropped out of my head when I saw my room.

A king-sized bed took up most of the space, but to the right of the bed was a nook with a towering window, thick navy blue curtains for privacy, and an ash brown, solid wood desk that looked like it came out of an antique store. The wallpaper was the same shade as the curtains, with cream flowers covering it in an asymmetric pattern. Plush, off-white carpet covered the room, which I was thankful for. I didn't want to get splinters when I was getting up at night to pee. Speaking of…

"Where's the bathroom?" I peered back into the common room, but didn't see extra doors.

"That's the first question everyone asks," Alisa explained. "We have a communal bathroom down the hall to the right. It's kind of a pain, but it's supposed to promote 'community.'"

She put air quotes around the word, and I wondered exactly what kind of person I would be rooming with for the next nine months.

My mom hoisted my tattered suitcase off the floor and plopped it on the bed. "That will be nice," she said a little too cheerily, "You'll get to mingle with all the other girls."

She knew I didn't want to be here, and she was trying to sell me on the place.

"Just the ones on this floor." Alisa corrected.

Mom faced Alisa and asked the single most embarrassing question of my life. "These dorms aren't co-ed, are they? I didn't see another building when we entered the school."

Alisa turned the charm up to a hundred. "No, ma'am. The boys' dorm is on the other end of the campus. Even though all the living quarters are in one building, it's big enough where the faculty isn't concerned about co-mingling after curfew. We have a few other structures around the property, but they're used for classes and extracurriculars. In fact, the school doesn't allow anyone in the dorms during the school day without permission, and at night we have security patrol the halls."

Mom looked impressed and started asking Alisa a million other questions about how good the security was and about the academics. I tuned it out and went back into the common room. The rain pattered on the window softly, and the flickering of the fire complemented the sound. My body began relaxing as I took a seat in a springy antique armchair and watched as two raindrops on the window raced each other. I had to admit the scenery was incredible. Tall trees surrounded the campus, and their leaves were turning vibrant hues of yellow and orange. They weren't at their peak color yet, but it would be breathtaking when they were. I could see some of the buildings in town through the branches, and their brick facades once again seemed to complement everything else around them. This school — this town — really was picture perfect.

"Ophelia?" Mom called. "It's about time I leave."

I turned my attention away from the gloomy atmosphere and peered at my mom. I stretched and walked her out of the dorm. She gave me a hug and kissed my cheek, and I watched her retreating figure disappear with the realization that this was now my life.

Once my mom was out of sight, Alisa pulled me back into the dorm and gave me a sly smile.

"Okay, now that the parental figure is gone, let me give you the actual lowdown of this place because it's awesome!"

Alisa gushed about all the weekend parties the boys' wing throws because none of the security actually gave a crap that students were mingling, which teachers were hot or not (I didn't care, but Alisa was an energetic talker), and all the cool hangout spots in town, including a tiny spiritual shop run by an elderly man.

After a half hour of her talking, and me giving the occasional nod or "mhm" there was a knock on the door. Alisa squealed and ran to answer it. After a brief minute, she ushered in a shy-looking girl with her parents in tow. Dark brunette hair flowed down her back in a low ponytail, and her round glasses caught the light of the chandelier overhead as she repositioned the rims back on her nose. Her roaming, deep blue eyes popped against her fair complexion. I guessed this was Bethany, our other roommate.

Alisa gave Bethany's parents the tour of the dorm that she had given my mother while Bethany stood awkwardly in the middle of the common room, looking anywhere but at me. I rose and extended my hand toward Bethany.

"Hi, I'm Ophelia."

Bethany gave me a small smile and wrapped her fingers around mine cautiously. "I'm Bethany Woods. It's nice to meet you."

Her hand felt fragile, as if grabbing something too quickly would shatter her bones.

"You too," I agreed. "You can put your bag down and make yourself comfortable."

She dropped my hand and clutched her book bag tighter to her body, like a shield. She didn't say another word, and I understood. Being in a new place was tough, especially if you didn't know anyone. Like me. I settled myself on the couch again next to the fireplace and took comfort in the warmth of the flickering flame.

Bethany looked above my head, and her demeanor changed. She looked... scared. I looked up at the portrait and back at Bethany.

"Creepy, isn't he?" I asked in a stage whisper.

She nodded, and I saw her body relax ever so slightly. Alisa returned to the common room, having finished the "grand tour" for Bethany's parents. She grabbed Bethany's wrist like she had mine earlier and nearly dragged her into the room on the far left. I just watched the fire and waited for them to be done.

A cold, whispered voice blew through the room like a winter breeze, chilling me to the bone. I jumped off the couch and whirled around in every direction, trying to find where it came from. When I found nothing, I shook off the discomfort as best I could and paced the common room, waiting for Alisa, Bethany, and her parents to emerge. When they finally did, the room felt warm again, like nothing had happened, and maybe nothing had. I chalked the whisper up to first-day nerves as Bethany's parents gave her hugs and kisses, promised to call her when they were home, and left.

Bethany looked like she wanted to crawl inside herself. I almost wanted to do the same, but Alisa clapped her hands and told us to get dressed (even though I thought both me and Bethany already looked presentable) and meet back in the common room in half an hour.

"Why?" I asked.

Alisa gave me a grin so devilish I thought she just might *be* the devil. "Because," she said, "we're going to a welcome party."

Chapter Two

THE WELCOME PARTY WAS certainly... a party. With loud thumping music shaking the walls, and flimsy red cups in every teenager's hand, however, it didn't make me feel very welcome. I imagined Bethany thought the same thing because if I didn't know any better, I would have thought she was trying to make herself seem smaller. Which would have been a feat because she was about five foot three and so slim it looked like she would blow away with a strong enough wind. She tucked a strand of her now loose hair behind her ear and pushed her glasses up her nose.

I wandered into the room, weaving through and behind people who were either dancing or just milling about. I needed a drink, preferably soda, so I glanced around, trying to find anything that resembled a two-liter. Nothing. You'd think a party like this would at least have soda for mixing drinks. I was about to give up when someone shoved a half-empty plastic bottle in front of my face with fizzy brown liquid sloshing inside.

"You look like you could use this."

I turned around and found a very tall and extremely hot boy standing in front of me. I looked up at his full height, and his striking silver eyes gazed down at me. His full lips curled at the corner as he offered me the bottle again. Well, I did say I wanted a drink. I grabbed the bottle by the neck and chugged three big gulps. The boy looked impressed and smiled so wide a row of perfectly white teeth showed through his full lips, and for a moment, I wondered what it would be like to kiss him.

"Dorian Whitmore,"

"Hm?" I turned my attention back to reality and hoped he hadn't noticed me staring.

He leaned in, his breath tickling my ear. "My name. Dorian Whitmore."

A shiver ran through me. I wanted to lean into his voice. It was soft and smooth, like velvet. And damn, he smelled good. Like he had just come from a rigorous run through the surrounding forest. Crisp, musky, and earthy all at once. Dorian stepped back and eyed me with a mischievous twinkle in his eye.

"What?" I asked.

He chuckled and crossed his arms. "Am I that earth-shatteringly gorgeous that I leave you speechless?"

Yes.

"No." My tone was a little too defensive. "I think I'm just getting a little tired."

While not the entire truth, the party *was* getting a little overwhelming. Dorian pursed his lips and extended an arm. "Come on then," he said, "I'll walk you back to your dorm. And maybe on the way, you can tell me your name."

I took his hand, and it felt like ten thousand volts of electricity ran through me. From his wide eyes, I guessed he felt it too, but he headed for the door without saying a word, leading me away from the noise of the bass and the chatter.

"Wait," I called, "I came here with my roommates. Bethany and Alisa."

Dorian scoffed. "Alisa will be here all night, so don't worry about her. As for your other roommate..."

Dorian glanced around the room, flexing his fingers around mine.

"I don't see her," he continued. "Maybe she already left."

He shrugged and led me away from the festivities again. He took hall after hall, like he knew exactly where he was going, the music growing softer with every step. We didn't stop until we were staring at the door to my dorm.

"How did you —"

Dorian gave me a mischievous wink and rapped his knuckles on the door twice before letting my hand go.

"Goodnight, Ophelia," he said as he sauntered away.

"Wait!" I called after him. "I never gave you my name."

He shoved his hands in his pockets and shrugged. "I know."

My mouth hung wide, and I was about to go after him when the opening of the door sounded and I turned my attention to Bethany, who already had her pj's on. She rubbed her eyes like she had been asleep.

"Why did you knock?" she asked, "the door was open."

My mind was still reeling, and my only response was, "Sorry. I didn't think."

She nodded sleepily as I strolled in. Bethany closed the door behind her and wobbled to the couch. A thick book lay on the floor alongside it, its copper-colored cover splayed open.

Bethany picked the novel up, dusting it off as she flumped onto the couch with a heavy sigh. I sat next to her and curled my legs up to my chest.

"How was the party?" Bethany asked.

I shrugged. "It was okay. It's been a while since I've been to a party."

She clutched the book tighter to her body. "I've never actually been to a party like that before. I didn't like it."

"Too loud?"

Bethany nodded.

"I understand. Parties aren't my scene anymore either." My chin rested against my knees. "I haven't felt very social lately."

My eyes closed, and the horrific memory flashed through the back of my eyelids, branded in my memory.

I snapped my eyes open, and the sharp inhale made Bethany's face scrunch.

I stood up and waved off the inevitable question, making my way to the foreign cell that was my new bedroom.

Flicking on the table lamp on my nightstand, I lifted my tattered suitcase off the bed and set it by the wardrobe. I flung myself onto the soft mattress and melted. It felt like I was sinking into an immense marshmallow.

I curled under the covers and sighed. The surge of images and sounds from the never-ending nightmare wouldn't go away. I couldn't shake the tightening in my chest, or the urge to give myself over to the tears that had been threatening to fall ever since the cops knocked on our door three months ago. I turned toward the window. The curtains were still open, and only pitch black greeted me outside the window. Rain pattered against the glass in a soothing stream. I closed my eyes, listening to the sound, and drifted into the beckoning darkness.

Muted light filtered through the window and woke me. I stretched my muscles, momentarily forgetting where I was, but the events of yesterday rushed back. Throwing off the feathery duvet, I padded to the window and eyed the gray clouds hanging overhead, making the trees of the New Hampshire landscape faded, yet somehow even more vibrant.

A groan escaped my throat as I shuffled over to my suitcase. Classes started tomorrow and since all I pulled out from the mangled mess of multicolored fabric was a wrinkled purple shirt, and some inside-out black jeans, it was time I unpacked.

With my clothes on and smoothed out, I tied my sneakers and left my room. Bethany was curled up on the couch, reading the same book I had seen on the floor last night. She didn't even glance at me as I wandered over and perched on the cushion next to her. I tugged at a piece of my pin-straight, sandy blond hair, and bit my bottom lip.

Bethany peered at me over the top edge of her book.

"Yes?" she asked.

Clearing my throat, I said, "I wanted to apologize for last night. I never intended to brush off your questions."

"It's okay," Bethany said. "We barely know each other. You don't owe me anything."

I shrugged. "I know, but since we're roommates, we're going to have to get along, and I didn't want you to think that I didn't like you or anything."

Bethany maneuvered herself on the couch so she was still curled up but facing me fully. "I don't think that. In fact, I was worried you might think I didn't like you, which is not true. I'm just not very good in new situations."

"Me either, honestly," I said.

A pit formed in the bottom of my stomach. It wasn't the truth. Not entirely, anyway. I had never been good at opening up around people. My dad said it was because I was a rose waiting for the right conditions to bloom, but Mom thought it was because I never took a chance to trust people. And I wanted to trust people. I wanted to bloom. So I took a deep breath and held it for a moment, and when the breath left my lungs, I tucked my feet under me so I faced Bethany head-on as well.

"Something happened," I explained, "back home. It messed me up, and ever since, it's been... hard."

She closed the book and set it in her lap. "Something bad," she guessed.

I nodded. I opened my mouth to explain more, but the words wouldn't come out. After the third time trying to speak, I knew I couldn't open up.

So, I shook my head and muttered, "Never mind."

Bethany's blue eyes filled with compassion. "You can tell me when you're ready. If you still want to."

My whole body went slack, releasing the tension that had built up, and I smiled my thanks. Alisa threw open her bedroom door, making Bethany and me jump, and that was the end of that conversation.

"Good morning, all!" she cheered.

Ugh, Alisa was a morning person. This year was going to be hell.

"Morning," I grumbled.

Bethany smiled and nodded in her direction, returning to her reading. Alisa took one look at both of us and decided we needed coffee. Bethany and I looked at each other and shrugged. I didn't particularly like coffee, but I doubted they had a soda fountain. I needed to know where the cafeteria was, anyway, so Bethany and I begrudgingly followed Alisa downstairs.

The cafeteria was enormous, and very Ivy League chic. Long mahogany tables lined both sides of the room, and at the very back was the buffet line filled with various steaming breakfast foods. There weren't many people down here either because it was too early, or because not everyone had arrived on campus yet.

Alisa rushed to a table in the corner that housed the industrial-sized coffee maker and Styrofoam cups. I shuffled to the food and grabbed a plate. The smell of everything in the buffet line made my stomach grumble greedily. I grabbed a freshly made Belgian waffle (because who wouldn't?) and slathered it in butter and syrup — the real kind — and walked over to the furthest corner of the room where Bethany had chosen a table. Her head was once again in her book. I wasn't a big reader, but Bethany seemed like she couldn't put it down. I needed to ask her why it was so interesting.

Alisa joined us a moment later and sighed contentedly when she brought the disposable cup of dark liquid to her lips. After a few sips, she looked even more alert than she had when we had woken up, which I didn't think was possible.

"So," Alisa said, eyeing me as I took a big bite of waffle, "I saw you talking to *the* hottest guy in school last night at the party."

"Who?" The question came out muffled because I was still chewing my waffle.

"Dorian Whitmore! He's only the hottest, most popular guy in this school. Hell, he's the hottest, most popular guy in *town*."

I gulped down my waffle with a swig of orange juice I had picked up on the way over to the table. "Why should I care about that?"

Bethany's head still angled toward her book, but her eyes were on me and Alisa.

Alisa huffed dramatically and continued to explain to me how being popular was the greatest thing ever. I didn't care, but what she said next piqued my curiosity.

"And," she said, "being notable is your one-way ticket to join The Divine Order."

"What's that?" Bethany said, finally looking up.

Alisa waved us closer as she peered around the room before speaking in a stage whisper.

"The Divine Order is the one club in this school you can't sign up for. You need to be invited in, and it's tres exclusive. No one is supposed to know about it, but it's kind of like this town's open secret."

I rolled my eyes and leaned back in my seat, flipping my hair over my shoulder. "A secret society of elite teenagers and nepo babies? No thanks."

Bethany hummed in agreement. I had to admit, a secret society sounded kind of cool, but not if it meant I would have to slum it with people who thought they were better than everyone just because they had money.

Alisa just shrugged and crossed her arms. "Fine, but don't come crying to me when you both become the bottom of the high school food chain."

"I won't," I said.

Alisa narrowed her eyes at the comment but said nothing. Bethany excused herself a few minutes later, and Alisa and I made idle chitchat about what classes I had tomorrow, but the conversation was tense. I felt a strange presence behind me, and I swiveled in my chair to find Dorian Whitmore staring down at me, smirking.

"Hey Bubbles," he said, "mind if I have a seat?"

He didn't wait for my answer before scooting the chair next to me out and sitting down. Alisa gazed at Dorian wistfully, but I caught an edge of disdain. The expression was so brief I had to have imagined it.

"Waffles aren't very nutritious, Bubbles," Dorian said.

I sighed. "Your point? And stop calling me Bubbles. I'm not a Powerpuff Girl."

"I like *The Powerpuff Girls.*"

The legs of my chair screeched as I pushed it away from the table. Dorian's hand gently landed on my knee before I could get up.

"I'm sorry," he said. "I didn't mean to offend you."

I hesitated only briefly before I positioned myself back at the table, catching yet another seething glare from Alisa. What was her problem? I brushed it off, as there was a bigger issue that needed attention.

"You can take your hand off me now," I said.

"What?" Dorian knit his eyebrows.

I raised mine and peered down at his hand, which still rested on my knee.

"Oh," was all he said before removing his hand and repositioning it on his own lap.

I returned my attention to Alisa and tried to ignore Dorian altogether. "With tomorrow being my first day of classes, and you being my Peer Patron, will you show me where I need to go?"

Alisa, unsuccessfully, hid a sneer behind a smile.

"I'll take her to her classes tomorrow, Alisa," Dorian interjected. "Why don't you take your other roommate, Bethany, right? I'm sure she could use a guide as good as you."

Alisa's nose wrinkled as she plastered that same ingenuous smile on her face and nodded. We both ignored the response.

"Actually," Dorian twisted to face me fully. "Why don't I take you on a tour of the grounds today? That way, you'll know exactly where everything is and impress your geography teacher with your knowledge of directions."

I studied his eyes. They seemed stormy today. Less bright silver and more of a dull gray, and he had dark circles under them. His hair, which I thought was jet black yesterday but was actually more of a dark brown, had a disheveled appearance. Strands were sticking up in all different directions, like he had been running his hands through it vigorously. He seemed like he'd had a rough night, and since there had just been a party, he probably did. He still held himself with the self-righteous swagger I had seen the night before, though, which annoyed me.

"No, thanks." I stood and carried my tray to the trash can before walking out without so much as another peek in his direction.

I spent the rest of the day in my room cursing everything. My mother, the town, this school, and freaking Dorian Whitmore.

Chapter Three

D AMN HIM.

Dorian was right about me getting turned around, even though I didn't want to admit it. The school itself was a single building, but it was enormous, with various wings and staircases going in every direction. Trying to navigate it while every other new student was trying to do the same? It was chaos. I was bumping into people left and right because I was trying to focus on where I was going, peer at my schedule, and search the halls for the right classrooms simultaneously. I was just thankful that I had gotten up somewhat early and found my way back to the cafeteria, because from the chatter I overheard in the halls, not everyone got to eat this morning.

First period was in a classroom at the very back of the ground floor, and I barely made it on time. With a heavy sigh, I slouched down in one of the empty desks in the back and tried to slow my breathing. The frantic search did nothing for my already frayed nerves. I reached into my book bag and pulled out a battered card, reading it again, as I had every day for the past three months, hoping this time it would comfort me. I stashed it back in my bag as the bell rang and the teacher called for attention.

Raven's Cove Academy's brochure hadn't been lying when it said the school was all about the academics. The teacher, I already forgot his name, spent the first five minutes of class having us introduce ourselves (which felt like literal torture), but then it was right to work. By the time the bell rang signaling the end of the hour, my head was swimming, and the homework sat heavy in my binder.

Second and third periods were much the same way. Five minutes for introductions, and then right to the lesson. By the time lunch rolled around, I had algebraic equations and dates of historic events swirling around in my brain, and I swear I was starting to confuse the two.

The cafeteria was nothing like it had been the day before. Where it had been quiet yesterday, today students crowded the extensive area, milling about, getting food, chatting with new friends and old. The sound alone made my muscles freeze and a cold pit grow in my stomach.

I looked around for Bethany or Alisa but faces blurred together. I couldn't think. My heart beat faster, the room was getting hot, and the floor swayed beneath my feet. A cool hand gripped my upper arm and kept me from falling. This person tugged me out of the cafeteria and kept pulling until crisp air greeted me, and my lungs rapidly filled with the fresh air. Whoever had led me outside let go, and I put my hands on my knees, steadying myself. My breathing became normal, and my pounding heart slowed.

"Thanks." I straightened and gaped at the smirk of the guy who saved me from a humiliating first day of school and groaned.

I rolled my eyes as Dorian said, "No problem, Bubbles."

He ran his hand through his dark hair nonchalantly, the midday sun catching some strands, giving them a slightly golden hue. His face, by comparison, was anything but. Dorian's eyes were dull and distant. He bit his bottom lip, and his throat bobbed as he swallowed. I knew that expression. I had seen it so many times since the funeral. It was the look of disappointment and disgrace. It was the look of *pity*, and it enraged me.

A loud screech ripped from my lungs as I marched away from him and the school. He caught up with me easily since he was much taller, and therefore, had longer legs. Curse being short.

"I'm fine," I snapped.

"Didn't ask."

I stopped short and pivoted toward him. "What do you want?"

He took a step back, his eyes wide and his palms up in a calming gesture.

"I wanted to make sure you were alright," he said. "I thought you were going to pass out back there."

"I'm fine," I repeated, my earlier anger subsiding for the moment. "I'm sorry."

"Me too."

I cocked my head to the side and took a couple of steps toward him. "Why are you apologizing?"

Dorian stuffed his hands in his pockets. "Because I feel like I pissed you off somehow."

I crossed my arms and tossed my hair over my shoulder. "No, you didn't *do* anything. You're arrogant, and I don't like arrogant people."

He cocked his head to the side, gave me a lopsided smile, and took a few steps toward me. He stopped only when our bodies were mere inches from each other. His hands were still in his pockets, but that same electric shock from last night ran through me, and I inhaled sharply. His scent invaded my nostrils, intoxicating me. It masked the smell of the surrounding forest, but his own woodsy scent replaced it.

He gently caressed my cheek with the back of his hand, his skin barely making contact, but it was enough to make my eyes flutter closed.

"Ophelia," he whispered.

My eyes snapped open, and I took several steps back. "You did that last night."

Dorian's face scrunched up. "Did what?"

"My name. You know my name, but I never said it."

Dorian ran his hand through his hair and sighed.

"I saw your file in the office when I was filling out some paper-work for Ms. Crane."

My heart stopped. "What did the file say?"

If the school file contained information about what happened… no. I couldn't let myself think that. I would just put myself into a panic.

Dorian ambled forward. "Honestly, not much. There was your name and a photo. That's it."

I wrapped a lock of hair around my finger. "You're sure?"

Dorian trudged forward again until he had closed the distance between us.

"I'm sure," he said.

I tugged at the hair, and Dorian's eyes fixed on the movement. He lifted his arm and took the strand in his own fingers, rubbing it between his pointer and his thumb.

"Your hair feels like silk." His voice was so low, I barely registered what he said.

The bell rang, signaling the end of lunch, and we both jumped at the sound. I had to swallow and clear my throat before I could speak.

"We should get back."

Dorian agreed, and we strolled toward the door that would lead us back into the school. Dorian snatched my arm after a moment and jerked me back tight into his chest. I yelped at the sudden action. He crossed his arms over my body like a cage, his grip on my torso tight enough to hurt.

We were both looking ahead, but Dorian's body was rigid. The gray clouds that roiled overhead seemed to darken, and the trees swayed with an invisible wind. The surrounding air grew heavy and cold, and I thought I saw a shadow move at the edge of the trees.

"Wha—" I started.

"Shh," Dorian hissed.

Something filled my ears with an ancient sound. The whispered voice I had heard when I first arrived slithered against my skin like a serpent, chilling me to my bones and making me shiver against Dorian's chest. It said something I didn't understand, and Dorian tightened his embrace even more.

A form of pure smoky shadow appeared in front of us. Vaguely humanoid, the figure glided forward.

"Get away from her. She is not yours." His tone was sharper than a razor, and almost as chilling as the earlier whispers.

The shadowy form slithered around, trying to find any way around Dorian's defense, but when it found none, it pointed at me and melted into nothing. After a moment, the sky returned to normal, and even though it was cool outside with the autumn air, it felt like spring compared to a second ago.

I struggled against my bonds, and Dorian released his hold on me. He paced in a circle while tousling his hair, making his intentionally messed up hairstyle even messier. My body shivered, and my teeth chattered. Wrapping my arms around myself, I tried to make sense of what I had just witnessed. Surely it had been a prank for the first day of school. Or what if it was worse? A whimper escaped from my lips. What if I was hallucinating? Dorian paused his pacing and gave me a wary glance. After several moments of opening and closing my mouth like a fish, I found my voice.

"Wh... what was that?" I asked.

Dorian was as still as a statue. "What do you think it was?"

I threw my hands wide. "I don't know, that's why I'm asking you!"

My knees wobbled, and when I tried to take a step toward him, my legs gave out altogether. I hit the pavement hard, and pain sang through my legs. Pain that made what I just witnessed real. Warm tears flooded my eyes, and I started sobbing. Big, heavy sobs that made my throat hurt. I didn't know why I was crying. What I saw confused me, and maybe I was in shock, but I couldn't stop the tears that flowed down my cheeks onto the pavement.

Dorian knelt in front of me and gently pulled my chin up so I stared into blazing silver eyes that burned brighter than molten metal. He angled his head down and kissed my forehead. My tears stopped as I closed my eyes and leaned into the sensation. His lips were warmer than they should have been. The heat from the kiss spread through my body, and I felt heavy.

A nap sounded nice. Where was I? Darkness was pulling me down, and I thought I heard a smooth voice apologize, but I was already too far gone to respond.

The alarm on my phone blared, and I groggily turned over and grabbed it to hit snooze. My phone buzzed again, but it wasn't the alarm this time. I looked at who messaged me and I grumbled. Mom texted me asking how my first day of classes was. I didn't respond. Mostly because I couldn't remember. Weird. Classes must not have been that interesting.

I dragged myself out of the comfort of the cloud-like mattress and pulled some clothes out of the closet. I was pulling on black stockings when I noticed both of my knees were black and blue. When did I get bruises? And *how* did I get bruises? I brushed off the question and put on some tan slacks instead. The dress code here wasn't strict, but we had a uniform. Skirts or slacks and white or black button-down shirts with a blazer that was embroidered with the school crest. It wasn't my style, but I also didn't mind it. It was nice not to have to think about what I was going to wear every day.

The common area was empty when I came out of my bedroom. Alisa and Bethany were probably down in the cafeteria already, and food sounded amazing. I went down flight after flight of stairs, groaning and grunting with each bend of my knees. Students, some of whom were still in pj's, shuffled around the cafeteria. I looked for Alisa or Bethany but couldn't see either of them. There was an empty table near the food line, so I piled a plate full of turkey bacon and eggs and sat down.

I was almost finished wolfing down my food when three boys entered the cafeteria and I froze, a forkful of scrambled eggs suspended near my open mouth. There was a boy with light brown hair on the left who looked like old money raised him, and a boy with tawny brown skin with a beautiful golden undertone on the right joking around with a guy who had dark brown hair and striking silver eyes.

Those eyes darted through my mind, as if I had seen them somewhere. Flashes of terror pricked through the haze I had felt all morning. My mind tried to shake off the murkiness and focus, but it was almost like I ran into a wall when I tried.

Money Boy pointed to me and whispered something to Silver Eyes. They glanced in my direction. No, they stared right at me. Money Boy howled with laughter, while the boy with the handsome brown skin regarded me with what could have been sympathy. Silver Eyes watched me with a smirk and motioned to my fork. I looked down. It still hung in the air, a bite of scrambled eggs jiggling on the prongs. I dropped my hand hastily, the fork clattering against the plate, and eggs splattered all over. I brushed the rogue bits off my shirt, but when my eyes looked for the boys again, they were gone.

Classes passed by slowly. My mind kept thinking back to those eyes. I knew them, but I couldn't remember from where. Images danced in my head throughout the day. A shadow man, an icy wind, arms that kept me secure, but the more I tried to concentrate on those moments, the fuzzier they became, and the more my head ached.

The last bell rang, and I needed to find somewhere silent to clear my thoughts. So I headed to the one place like that I knew.

The school's library was larger than most of the classrooms combined, and I wasn't sure how it didn't take up half of the entire building. The walls were the same dark, wainscoted wood as everywhere else, and the ceilings were tall and vaulted with an intricate mural painted in muted, neutral tones that comple-mented the reddish-brown tones of the space. Archways lined either side of the massive room, branching off into tinier alcoves filled to the brim with bookshelves. Placed in the middle of the room were several long tables that looked like they belonged in a banquet hall rather than a library. Small lamps cast a warm glow from every table, and way in the back I saw a girl with brown hair braided over her shoulder and glasses that kept falling down her nose reading a thick book.

Bethany.

I made my way over to her and softly cleared my throat. Bethany peeked over the pages and smiled warmly.

"Mind if I sit here?" I asked.

"All yours." Bethany placed a bookmark in the pages and set the novel down.

I dragged the chair out, the legs scraping along the hardwood floor. I muttered an apology to the surrounding students, who shot daggers at me for the interruption, and sat down.

"What are you reading?" I asked.

Bethany's whole being sparked to life at the question, and she began telling me all about the characters and the plot. It was a fantasy about dragons, daring adventures, and a hot guy in leather. It honestly sounded intriguing. I interrogated her about it, asking about what happens, and how hot is the hot guy in leather. We talked for an hour just about her book. When she couldn't give me any more details (she hadn't finished the story), she began a line of questioning of her own.

"Dorian Whitmore seems to be captivated by you. How do you feel about him?"

A jolt went through my body at the mention of his name. The picture of a smug pale face with staggering eyes made of silver erupted through my head, but as soon as the image appeared, pain sliced through my skull. My fingers massaged my temples, and the pain subsided.

"I —" My mind was becoming hazy again, and the harder I tried to focus, the harder it was to remember. "I don't know who that is."

Bethany seemed to see my confusion. "Ophelia, are you okay?"

I nodded absentmindedly. Bethany reached across the table and gingerly shook my shoulder, pulling me back into reality, and suggested we go back up to the dorm. Alisa had a microwave in her room, and Bethany had swiped some packets of hot chocolate from the cafeteria.

"Hell, yes," I agreed, putting the thought of whoever's name behind me.

Chapter Four

CLASSES WERE SURPRISINGLY INTERESTING once I had half a mind to pay attention. We were three weeks into the semester and even though Bethany and I didn't have any classes together, we would go to the library every day to do homework and talk about Bethany's books. She had given me a couple to borrow, and I enjoyed them, though I had never been an avid reader. Bethany and I also found we had other common interests, and we became best friends.

When the weekends came, we would curl up on the couch in the common room and have movie marathons in our pj's. Bethany was really into period pieces like *Pride and Prejudice,* and since I was more of a rom-com girl, we would take turns showing each other different films and sharing random facts about our celebrity crushes.

Alisa was never in the dorm a lot. She was always at some party the boys' wing was throwing or doing something with her other friends. I had met one of them once. She had knocked on the door while Alisa was down the hall showering. The girl was picture-perfect. Like if a photo of a model had walked right off the page of a magazine with salon perfect brunette hair and flawless skin. She was a little snobby, though, and I came to realize over the weeks that Alisa was too. She was friendlier with Bethany than me, however, and I'm glad because aside from me, I didn't see Bethany hanging out with many people. I didn't have many friends at Raven's Cove Academy, either. There were a few people I would talk to in class, especially when we had group assignments, but I never hung out with any of them outside of the classroom. Once in a while, while I was walking through the halls or out in the courtyard, I would envision silver eyes, or catch a scent of crisp earth, and I would try to place them, but never could.

I was passing through the halls, going to my next class, when I spotted Bethany talking to someone. He was taller than she was, but lanky, with short, light brown hair and a stance that made me automatically dislike him. Bethany seemed to enjoy his company, though, because he leaned in and whispered something in her ear, and she actually turned red while she giggled. I didn't want to interrupt and embarrass either of them — or me — so I kept walking. I would press her for information later.

That day, after the last bell, I met up with Bethany in our usual spot in the library, but it was apparent that her conversation earlier still had her excited. Her eyes were roaming all over the room, and she wouldn't sit still.

"Okay, what's up?" I scooted the chair out and sat down.

"I don't know what you mean." Her eyes peeked past me, like she was waiting for someone.

I folded my arms on the table and leaned in. "I mean, I saw you talking to someone in the hall today, and now your entire personality has changed. You're bouncing all over the place, and —"

Bethany wasn't paying attention. I placed my hand on hers and she jumped.

"And now you're not even paying attention to our conversation."

Bethany's cheek flushed. "Yes, I am, and I talk to lots of people. You aren't my only friend."

I snorted. "You're more introverted than I am, unless you're talking to a tall boy with caramel brown hair. And you weren't just chatting with this person either. You were *flirting* with them. And from what I saw, he was flirting back. So spill."

Bethany's nose scrunched up with delight, and she grabbed the hand that was on top of hers. "Okay, I can't tell you everything right now, but he asked me out today."

I squeed loudly, and someone from a table over shushed me. I squeed more silently.

"For when?" I asked in a stage whisper.

Bethany leaned in so she could whisper, too. "This Friday. He invited me to one of the dorm parties."

I gave her a confused look. "You — but you hate parties."

Bethany shrugged. "I know, but he's really cute, and he said after the party there's like this sort of afterparty that only select people get to go to."

I snorted and leaned back. "An after-dorm-party party? That's... excessive."

Bethany laughed as she relaxed in her chair. "I know, but I really like this guy, Ophelia. And I think he really likes me, too."

"I'm so happy for you, Beth. So, do I get this guy's name or am I going to just keep calling him 'that guy' forever?"

Bethany smiled and put her finger to her lips. I scoffed, and she giggled.

"Okay, okay. His name is Joel Weston."

She said his last name like it should mean something. When I didn't speak up or ooh and ahh, she blinked.

"Do you not know who the Westons are?" she asked.

I shook my head. "Sorry, but no."

Bethany motioned me to sit next to her, and I moved seats. She scooted so close to me our knees were touching.

"The Westons are a really rich and super influential family. They pretty much own the east half of New Hampshire."

I nodded, but people with money never impressed me. It surprised me it mattered to Bethany.

We talked a little more about Joel, but when the conversation turned toward me and my nonexistent love life, I tried to steer the conversation to homework as casually as I could. Bethany's expression was skeptical, but she didn't push the topic, which I was extremely grateful for.

Several hours and about a thousand Spanish conjugations later, one of the library staff informed us we needed to head back to the dorm for curfew, so Bethany and I packed up our stuff and headed upstairs.

We were on the second floor when I noticed my phone wasn't in my pocket. I told Bethany to keep going as I turned around and headed back to the library. Only when I got there, the staff had already locked the doors. I knocked and knocked, but there was no answer. In desperation, I tugged on the door handles and groaned.

"Breaking and entering is hardly model student behavior."

I whirled around, and a hand covered my mouth before I could let out a shriek. The hand quickly moved, but I still stood speechless. The boy with silver eyes stood before me, and wow, they were even more striking up close. A flash of those same eyes entered my mind, along with the memory of loud music and a half-empty bottle of soda. Weird.

"Am I that handsome that I leave you speechless?"

An electric shock went through my mind, and my eyes widened.

"Wha-what did you say?"

The boy paled, like he had said something he shouldn't have.

"Nothing," he said quickly. "You should go back to your dorm."

He spun and was walking away when I called back, "But my phone's in there!" I stomped my foot, and the boy turned back toward me, crossed his arms, and smirked.

"Are you throwing a tantrum?" His bemused voice made me even more annoyed.

"No," I said. "I was just... showing my irritation."

"By throwing a tantrum." He swaggered back toward me.

I stuck my tongue out at him, and he bit his lip to keep from laughing. Sighing, I turned away from the boy to peer through the glass panes on the door, hoping to see a faculty member who had stayed late.

"Seriously, there's no one in there," the boy said. "You might as well head back upstairs, and search in the morning."

"I think that's an excellent idea."

We jumped at the sound of a deep voice coming from behind as a male figure stepped from what seemed directly out of the shadows. His face was sallow and sunken in, like he was incredibly sick, and his white hair was thin and dull.

"Headmaster Keswick." The boy gave a slight nod.

His entire posture had taken a one-eighty. Where he had been relaxed, and even smug, a second ago, his body was now rigid and his hands clenched into fists at his side.

"Hello, Dorian." The man turned his milky eyes to me. "And you are... Ophelia Allan, am I right?"

I swallowed before answering. "Yes, sir."

Headmaster Keswick rubbed his chin with a bony finger. "Hm. And Ophelia, you are aware it's after curfew, correct?"

I nodded. Every nerve in my body screamed at me to run, but I felt like Medusa had turned me to stone, and I was now frozen in place.

"Well then," he said, "I suggest you follow Mr. Whitmore's advice and go to bed. Walking the halls at night will get you into nothing but trouble. Especially if you're associating with Dorian here."

The headmaster looked pointedly at Dorian, who only straightened his already stiff stance and stared straight ahead of him.

"Yes, sir." I wanted to sprint upstairs, but I forced myself to walk. A frown formed on my face as I made my way back to my room, wondering why Dorian would be so afraid of such a frail man.

The next morning, I rushed to get dressed and headed down to the library to check for my phone. I got there just as the head librarian was unlocking the double doors. She held them open for me, and I gave her a rushed thank you as I jogged down to the end table Beth and I sat at the night before. My phone wasn't there. I looked in, on, under, and around the table and surrounding area, but my phone was nowhere to be found.

I asked the librarian if she had picked up my phone and when she told me she hadn't, the air got thicker, and I couldn't get as much oxygen into my lungs. That phone was the most important thing I had in my possession, and if I lost it, I didn't know what I would do.

I noticed the panic setting in, and I sat down in a cushy armchair next to an alcove of books and focused on my immediate surroundings, just like my therapist told me to. I found five things I could see. A red book, a tree with orange leaves out the window. Shifting my focus to touch, I ran my hands over the surface of the chair, and my clothes, feeling the texture and temperature of each object my skin connected with. Gentle ticking from the clock at the front of the library, and students making their way to the cafeteria waded into my ears. Taking a deep breath in, the scent of old books and the faint smell of bacon wafting in from the breakfast line hit my nostrils. Finally, I popped a mint I always kept in my bookbag in my mouth and focused on the sharp coolness coating my tongue.

The urge to panic was gone, and I could think a lot clearer. Logic told me I had simply misplaced my phone, and it was probably up in the dorm somewhere. I decided I would search after classes and headed down the last two flights of stairs from the library to get something to eat.

I found Bethany in the cafeteria, sitting and giggling with Joel. They sat so close together I thought Beth would end up on the guy's lap. I smiled at their obvious attraction to each other and grabbed some oatmeal from the back. Alisa noticed me and ushered me over. I glanced at her warily but sat down next to her. Her friend Rachel, the brunette I had met earlier, gave me a once-over and continued eating without saying a word.

"Don't mind her," Alisa rolled her eyes. "She's not a morning person."

Rachel scoffed. "I'm not an ugly person kind of person."

I raised an eyebrow and pursed my lips, but Alisa put her hand on my arm. "Seriously, she hasn't had her coffee yet."

I felt the table move and Rachel yelped.

"Right," she said, "I'm a bitch without my coffee."

I gave Alisa a small, awkward smile and picked at my oatmeal, which had sounded more appetizing when I first picked it up.

The warning bell rang a few minutes later, and I was grateful that I no longer had to sit in an awkward silence.

Normally I enjoyed my classes, but today they dragged on forever. After the last bell, I hauled ass to my dorm and started the frantic hunt for my phone. I flipped cushions and stuck my hand into crevices that probably hadn't been cleaned since the school first opened, and after tearing through every room like a tornado, there was still no sign of my phone.

Alisa and Bethany shuffled into the common room as I was putting the last cushion on the couch back into place. I asked them if either of them had seen my phone, and neither of them had. I sank into the newly fluffed couch and huffed. Bethany sat down beside me, and Alisa went into her room and locked the door.

"You might just have to tell your mom you lost it," Bethany said.

"It's not that," I said. "That phone has important photos on it and if I don't find it—"

My voice caught, and my bottom lip quivered.

Bethany grabbed my hand and squeezed gently. "You don't have to be in control of your emotions all the time, Ophelia. Sometimes, it's good to let it out."

"It's my fault," I whispered.

Bethany cocked her head to the side. "Your fault you lost your phone?"

"No." I could feel the dam of tears I had held back overflow, and I squeezed my eyes shut.

I couldn't break down. I couldn't bring myself to acknowledge what had happened, because if I did, Bethany would know what a horrible person I was, and she would hate me.

Everyone would hate me.

So, I just shook my head and chewed on my bottom lip. Bethany squeezed my hand once more and didn't push any further.

"I'm here if you need me." She rose from the couch and went to her room, leaving me alone in front of the cold fireplace and the founder of the academy's portrait looming over me.

Chapter Five

A THUNDERSTORM BLEW THROUGH that night, and if I wasn't already tossing and turning from the flashing images of red and blue lights in my mind, I would have been tossing and turning from the cracks of thunder that literally shook the windows. I gave up trying to sleep at half past two and padded down the hall to the bathroom.

I didn't expect anyone to be in there at this time of night, but light filtered through a small slit in the door, and when I heard whispered voices echoing into the hallway, I halted. People were not what I wanted to deal with right now, and I was just about to go back to the dorm until I heard Bethany's name. And not in a friendly way.

"Are you sure she's right for this?" a familiar voice asked.

"A young, gullible introvert? Of course she's right for it." This voice was deeper than the first.

What was a guy doing in the girl's bathroom?

"I just hope you know what you're doing, Joel."

Joel? Bethany's Joel?

"It's been too long since the last one," the girl continued, "and if we wait any longer, he'll…"

Her voice trailed off, but Joel responded a moment later.

"Rachel, baby, she's the perfect fit. Trust me. Now stop worrying, or you'll start looking as wrinkly as he is right now."

I couldn't hear anymore. With my need to pee forgotten, I rushed back down the hall as quickly and silently as I could. Shutting the door, the cool metal knob jabbed into the small of my back as I tried to make sense of what I had just overheard. Rachel and Joel? Were they together? What were they talking about? Who was *he*? Another boom of thunder sounded, and my heart skipped a beat. I trudged back to my room, crawled underneath the covers, and tried not to let my imagination run wild, even though it already was.

My dreams hated me that night. Staggering silver eyes and a disembodied voice that chilled me to the bone crept into my head even in my sleep. The alarm on the old analog clock Ms. Crane had lent me jerked me awake. I tried to get up, but I was so tangled in my covers that I ended up falling on the floor instead.

Cursing every inanimate object I could, I liberated myself from the sheets and went to find my uniform. I had taken a single step into the common area after getting dressed when Bethany greeted me in an unusually chipper manner. I staggered back a step, and she handed me a styrofoam cup with a lid. Grasping it, I took a sip and groaned. Coffee. My gag reflex wanted to expel the bitter liquid, but I didn't want to insult Beth. I shuffled behind her into the middle of the room. The fireplace was blazing, but the only one who knew how to light it was Alisa, and she didn't seem to be awake yet.

I flopped onto the couch, careful of the boiling hot drink in my hand. "Did you light the fire?"

Bethany nodded with fervor. "Joel taught me how to work the fireplace the other night. It was so romantic. We were in his dorm and —"

"Wait, when were you in his dorm?"

I must have still been asleep, because I swear I misheard that. We've been together every day this past week. I took a swig of coffee.

Bethany plopped down on the couch next to me, but it was like she couldn't sit still. She kept bouncing her leg like she was waiting for exam results. I took another gulp of coffee, fighting the grimace forming on my lips, and turned so I sat directly in front of her. Beth's hands fidgeted and she wouldn't meet my eyes.

"Beth?" I asked.

She finally glanced up and blushed. "I snuck out two nights ago and met Joel in his dorm. Nothing happened, we just talked in the common area, but it was so nice. Oh, Ophelia, I really like him!"

I gave her a small smile. I didn't enjoy breaking the rules like that, but then again, where have rules ever gotten me?

I squeezed her hand. "I'm really glad you like him. And he likes you back?"

She gave me another nod. The conversation I overheard last night echoed through my mind. I wanted to tell Bethany, but what if they weren't talking about her? I had seen Joel and Rachel interact in class, too. They seemed more like friends or siblings rather than a couple, and the last thing I wanted to do was hurt her unnecessarily.

So, I finished the rest of the coffee and threw the cup in the small trashcan in the corner. "He's going to have to pass the friend test, you know."

Bethany threw her arms around me and laughed. "No, he's going to have to pass the *best* friend test."

Those words made me hesitate for a moment, but I hugged her back fiercely. I've never had a best friend before. I mean, I had friends back home, but they all ignored me after what happened. It was like they knew it was my fault. I put that thought aside, and my body felt warm and weightless. I never wanted this feeling to go away.

We broke the hug, and Beth still seemed fidgety.

"What's with the jitters?" I asked.

Bethany blushed and looked down again. "It's Friday."

Oh! The after-dorm-party party. *That's* why she's a bundle of nerves.

"It's going to be fine," I said. "You two will have an amazing time."

She bit her lip. There was more.

"Are you okay, Beth?" I asked.

She motioned me forward, and I scooted closer to her so our knees were almost overlapping.

"I'm not supposed to say anything," she started, "but the after party on Friday is more of an initiation."

I leaned back. "An initiation? For what?"

She beckoned me closer again, and I complied. She put her lips to my ear, and spoke so softly I wasn't sure I heard her right.

"The Divine Order," she said.

I jerked back. "Really?"

"Yep!" Bethany beamed. "I met Joel's roommates the other day, and he told them I'd be a perfect fit!"

I was trying to wrap my head around what I had heard. "But — but why would you want to join a club like that?"

Beth's face fell. "I thought you'd be happy for me. I really like Joel, and this way he and I could spend so much time together. Not only that, but The Divine Order does so much good for the academy and the town. I want this."

I felt like an ass.

"Of course I'm happy for you, Beth. I just want to make sure this is what you really want to do."

"It is."

I plastered on the biggest smile I could. "Then I'm happy for you."

"You are?"

"Yes!" I said. "Now we should get going or we'll miss breakfast, and I get cranky when I've had no food."

Bethany and I were making our way out the door when I heard another door open from behind us. Alisa came out of her room looking extra put together. Her blonde hair was curled to perfection, and her makeup looked airbrushed on.

"If you guys are eating breakfast, you'd better wait for me." She grabbed Bethany's arm and pulled her out the door and toward the stairs, beaming at her. I followed and Bethany peered back at me in confusion. I shrugged, because honestly, Alisa being this nice to *anyone* seemed out of character for her.

The cafeteria buzzed with excitement. There had been dorm parties before, almost every weekend in fact, but this one was supposedly special because there was a full moon. Why that was special I didn't know, but I also didn't care enough to ask. The warning bell sounded about twenty minutes later, and I was grateful that I had gotten food, because while the students were rowdy, the teachers were extra cranky and weren't taking anyone's shit. Four people got detention in my morning classes alone.

By the time lunch rolled around, I just wanted the solitude of my room. Bethany, however, looked like she could barely contain her excitement when she sat down across from me, and it wasn't hard to know why. Joel scooted the chair out next to her and sat down. She looked at him, mesmerized. Alisa and Rachel sat down on either side of me a moment later and started chatting up Joel and Bethany. I had a feeling I was going to be eating lunch by myself, even if there were a bunch of people around me. Their conversation consisted mostly of how exhilarated everyone was for the party tonight, and the more they talked and laughed with each other, the more out of place I felt. The bell rang, signaling the end of lunch, and I didn't think I could be any more grateful for the shrill sound.

Afternoon classes were even worse than the morning classes. Six more students received detention, and by the time the bell rang, signaling the end of the school day, I was ready to go back to my dorm and relax. In my hurry, I didn't watch where I was walking and ran straight into someone, knocking their things to the ground. I stooped to pick up the books that had thudded to the ground.

"I'm so sorry," I said, "I wasn't watchi —"

My words left me as a pair of staggering silver eyes met mine. I swallowed and handed the books back to Dorian. He gently grabbed them from me and positioned them in the crook of his arm.

"I'm glad to see I still leave you speechless," he said.

It took me a few seconds to remember how to speak. "Hi."

Hi? Was that all my mind could muster up?

Dorian bit his lip to keep himself from smiling, but a small grin poked through.

"Hi," he said.

"I was just —" I jerked my thumb toward the stairs in an honestly horrible attempt to tell him where I was headed.

He nodded slowly. "Are you going to the party tonight?" His voice had a weird note to it, but I couldn't place why.

I shook my head.

"Good," he said too fast. "I mean, you look tired, and I wouldn't want you to lose your beauty sleep by staying up late with some drunken teenagers. Even if there will be soda there."

I raised my eyebrows. "Um, thanks. I think I'm going to go now."

I walked away before he could hurl another insult. I got to the dorm and Bethany greeted me while Alisa and Rachel fawned over her. Alisa had braided the top half of Bethany's hair and was now winding it around her head like a crown. Rachel was curling the loose bottom half of Beth's hair and securing the style with hairspray.

Bethany looked at me, and the sparkle in her eyes made me smile. She seemed so happy, but I couldn't help the nervous knot weighing on me in the pit of my stomach.

"Hey, Ophelia!" she called, "Want to help me pick out the outfit I'm going to wear?"

Rachel and Alisa locked eyes. It was clear I wasn't welcome at this makeover, even if Bethany wanted me to be. I wandered over to the three of them and gave Bethany a warm smile.

"I'm actually pretty tired, but I'm sure the girls have you covered. You look beautiful, Beth. Joel is going to die when he sees you."

That elicited a snicker from Rachel. Alisa smacked her on the shoulder, and I looked between the two of them, my brows furrowed. I looked at Bethany. The action made the knot in my stomach tighten, and I had to say something.

"Actually, Beth, I have something for you, but it's kind of special. Can you come to my room for a minute?"

Bethany jumped up and followed me, much to Rachel and Alisa's chagrin. I closed the door behind us and looked at Beth.

"Are you sure you want to go to this party tonight?" I asked. "We could just hang out here, maybe watch some movies and eat some popcorn."

Bethany frowned. "I already told you I want to go tonight. What's going on?"

I sighed. "I'm just worried that maybe..." How did I say it without her getting mad at me? "Maybe tonight won't go the way you think."

Bethany's frown deepened. "Ophelia, what's going on? Earlier you were so happy for me. Or so I thought."

I paced the floor in front of my bed. "I am, but I'm also worried. Alisa and Rachel don't really seem like the 'helping' type. So why are they doing your hair?"

Tears shone in Bethany's eyes. "Because they know tonight is special for me, and not just because of Joel. They're happy for me, and I'm sorry you aren't."

She started backing up toward the door. I reached for her.

"No, Beth, that's not what I—"

She shook her head and jerked out of my grasp. "Don't bother. You know, I actually feel sorry for you. You don't trust people enough to let them in. What happened back home that was so bad you can't talk to anyone about it? Even your supposed best friend."

Her next words hit me like a punch to the gut.

"I actually bet it was nothing, and you're just lying for the attention. It must be pretty exhausting to never let yourself be happy, and unlike you, I refuse to be that miserable."

She stalked out of the room, slamming the door behind her. I couldn't move. The dam burst open, and tears that I had kept under control for months rushed out and flooded my body.

The rest of the night was awful. I went to the bathroom after Bethany and the others left for the party, and at least a dozen girls crowded around the mirrors, getting ready. People weren't kidding when they said this party was different from the other ones the boys' wing had thrown. By the time I got my turn in the showers, all the hot water was gone. My groan turned into a yelp as the icy water hit my back. I quickly sped through washing my body and hair. There were no open dressing rooms, so I zipped back to my dorm in nothing but a towel, grateful that hardly anyone saw me.

I got into my fuzziest pj's and sank into the chair at my desk. The sun was barely above the horizon, making the sky light up with brilliant hues of orange and purple. I took my World History textbook out of my bag and tried to focus on my essay about the French Revolution, but after five minutes of my mind wandering, I slammed the book shut.

After fifteen more minutes of trying to find something, *any-thing*, to occupy my mind, I decided to just curl up and go to sleep. I cursed the fact that I still hadn't been able to find my phone so I couldn't listen to music while I fell asleep, but the sounds of crickets chirping outside made my body relax enough for me to slip into unconsciousness.

Sunlight shone through my window the next morning, waking me. I rushed out of bed and started hurriedly putting on my uniform until I remembered it was Saturday. I took a deep breath and tried to calm my racing heart. Since I was already out of bed, I threw on some jeans and a turtleneck and headed down for some breakfast.

My feet slowed as I passed by Bethany's door. I wanted — no, I *needed* — to apologize to her. She needed to know I am happy she found someone, and that hesitation had nothing to do with her. She needed to know what happened all those months ago. I pivoted toward the dark worn wood of her bedroom door, and knocked lightly.

No answer, but the door inched open slightly, and what I saw made me stop breathing.

Large drops of dark red trailed into the room from the opening. I cracked the door a little more, and on the floor by the bed, deep crimson covered the cream-colored carpet. This time it wasn't tiny droplets, but a huge shiny pool of liquid that rippled as more of the viscous substance dripped into it. My eyes followed the dripping to the source, and a strange sound came from my lungs, primal and desperate.

Sprawled on the bed, arms wide, was Bethany, her head hanging over the side of the mattress at an awkward angle. Her mouth was open like someone, or something, had scared her to death, and her blue eyes had glassed over. More of the dark liquid caked her brown, disheveled hair. Sticky strands poked out of the braid that tilted askew around her head, and gore glued the rest of her long hair to the sides of her neck. Or what was left of it, because the source of the syrup-like substance all over the room was a wide gash where someone had slashed Bethany's throat wide open.

I moved toward her without thinking. I was maybe a foot from her and I reached my arm out. Another scream filled the space, but this time it wasn't mine. I whirled to find Alisa staring at Bethany, her hand covering her mouth and tears in her wide eyes.

"Call 911." My voice sounded as hollow as Bethany's neck.

Alisa stood still and continued staring.

"Call an ambulance!" I screamed, my throat protesting from the action.

Alisa flinched but fumbled in her purse for her phone. She dialed with shaking fingers as I turned back around and fell to my knees, not caring that I landed in the pool of what I now knew to be blood. It felt like an eternity that I stared into Bethany's milky, lifeless eyes, but eventually someone hauled me to my feet. As I was being led away, I noticed something out of the corner of my eye. A symbol. Carved into Bethany's palm.

And as I was being escorted out of the dorm by a police officer, I noticed a boy with dark brown, messy hair — Dorian, standing there with his staggering silver eyes — staring at me, and I remembered everything from that horrid first day of school.

Chapter Six

Ashton's police station was small and had a reception desk, one holding cell directly across from it, and one interview room, where I currently sat.

A detective sat opposite me, thrumming his rich brown fingers on the cool metal of the sterile-looking table. The sound was the only thing keeping me in the present instead of sucking me into the past. I looked down at my hands, sticky with drying blood.

Bethany's blood.

I took a deep breath, the metallic smell stinging through my nostrils, held it for a minute, and let it out slowly. The detective, Russo, I think he said his name was, stopped tapping his fingers, and flipped open a folder that sat in front of him. It took some effort, but I finally looked at him. Pitch black braids hung in front of slanted, bushy brows. Gray-green eyes followed my every movement, and with each passing second, his lips pursed even more.

"Are you going to say something?" I asked.

"I'm waiting." His voice was deep and devoid of any emotion.

"For what?"

The room was chilly, and I wrapped my arms around myself as I shivered. Who in New England keeps the air conditioner on in the fall?

Detective Russo laced his fingers together on the table. "For you to spin some ridiculous story about your... friend's death."

He said "friend" like he didn't really believe Bethany and I had been friends.

"I don't know what you're talking about." My voice sounded small compared to his. So meek and unsure.

He scoffed and leaned back in his chair. "Playing innocent? Okay. Let me tell you what I know, and you can fill in the blanks, hm? I know that according to your roommate, you and Miss Woods had a disagreement yesterday, and that argument was about a boy. Were you jealous? I also know you were the one to find her body this morning, and isn't it convenient that no one saw you at all after you two had that spat? So, now it's your turn. Tell me why you killed her."

My hands fell limp at my sides, and I think my mouth actually popped open. "I — what?"

"Did she say some mean things to you? Were you upset? Did her comments drive you over the edge?" His tone was getting louder and sharper with every question. "What was it that made you snap?"

I couldn't believe what I was hearing. He actually thought I killed Bethany?

"I didn't... kill my best friend."

Detective Russo's mouth quirked to the side. "Are you feeling so guilty that you can't even say her name?"

"No, I —"

The weight of what he was accusing me of sank in. I opened and closed my mouth several times before any sound came out.

"Do I need a lawyer?"

Detective Russo cocked his head to the side, causing some of his braids to fall in front of his face. "Why would you need a lawyer? We're just having a conversation, and if you have nothing to hide, it shouldn't matter, anyway."

I couldn't move. My body felt frozen, and even the chill from the blowing vent above my head didn't register. I looked down at the stainless-steel table, unable to meet his eyes.

"I...didn't...kill...her." My voice sounded empty. Too far away where I didn't think I would ever find it again.

"Then why did we find your phone, smashed, next to her body?"

Detective Russo set a clear plastic baggie in front of me. Inside was indeed my phone, the screen shattered, mottled with blood.

My head snapped up. "I lost my phone a couple of days ago. I swear I don't know how it ended up in Bethany's room."

He snatched the baggie away. "Let's retrace your steps, then. Where were you last night at around midnight?"

I rubbed my hands down my blood-soaked jeans. "I felt awful after Beth and I had that fight and I couldn't concentrate on homework, so I went to bed early."

Detective Russo thumbed through the file and took a sharp breath in. He closed the file and looked at me.

"This isn't your first time finding a body." His voice had a hint of sympathy in it.

I stopped breathing. "No. Please don't go there. I didn't do it."

I could feel myself being pulled back in time. Coming home from my last day of my freshman year, unlocking the door, and... No.

I squeezed my eyes shut and returned to the present moment. Detective Russo was studying me. His eyes were softer, but only minimally.

"What I can't understand is why carve some... symbol into her hand? Why copy that?" he asked.

I was about to ask what he meant by "copy" when the door to the room swung open and the officer who escorted me here walked in. He whispered something to Detective Russo and left. The detective sighed and gathered the file.

"Miss Allan," Detective Russo said, "you're free to go. For now." He pointed a finger in my direction and narrowed his eyes. "But don't think you're off my radar."

I stood up, grateful that I didn't have to sit through any more questions, and stiffly shuffled out of the interrogation room. Detective Russo caught me by the wrist as I moved past him and leaned down.

"You may have friends in high places, Miss Allan," he said, "but trust me, the cost isn't worth whatever you're getting in return."

I peered up at him, his eyes full of desperation and pain.

"What are you talking about?" I asked.

Detective Russo merely shook his head and freed my wrist. I scurried past him and ran to the officer who brought me here, who was waiting to escort me back to Raven's Cove Academy. The ride was quick, and as soon as we pulled in front of the gates, I wanted to run. Away from the fact that my best friend was dead. Away from this school, and away from my life. A pair of silver eyes waiting by the entrance, however, made me rethink running.

I leapt out of the police cruiser as soon as it stopped, and I stalked up to Dorian. I opened my mouth to scream at him, but I wasn't sure what I was going to scream at him about. Bethany, the shadow form that confronted us on the first day of school, or that he had apparently wiped my memories from that day.

Dorian gripped my hand tightly before I could utter a sound and subtly glanced behind me. I turned, and the officer had gotten out of his cruiser and was staring at us. Waiting. I turned back to Dorian and motioned for him to lead the way with my eyes.

He let go of my hand, but rested his palm on the small of my back to direct me up the steep stone steps and inside the academy. Anytime I tried to stop, his hand would gently nudge me forward until we had reached the stairs branching off to the girls' and boys' dorms. My body locked up. I couldn't go upstairs. I couldn't return to my dorm and pretend like everything was normal. That... that Bethany didn't die in there.

Dorian seemed to read my thoughts, or maybe my face just showed my terror, and he moved his hand from my back and laced my fingers through his.

"You're okay," he murmured. "Everything is going to be okay." He gently pulled me to the other side of the staircase, leading me up to the boys' dorms. We came to a set of large double doors, newer than the rest of the building seemed, but still blending in with the architecture. He opened the doors, and we stepped into the common area, which was bigger than the entirety of my dorm.

It looked similar to the common room we had, but also very different. The walls and floor were the same, but there was a grand piano in the furthest corner. Its black surface was so polished it reflected the overhead lights, and a pool table sat in front of the floor-to-ceiling windows.

Instead of a large portrait above the mantel, there was a giant TV, and nestled in front of the roaring fireplace was a black leather sofa with two armchairs in the same upholstery arranged on either side. The warmth from the flames spread throughout the room, and I hadn't realized how cold I was until I was shivering so violently, I thought my bones would dismantle themselves like Legos.

Dorian strolled through a dark wooden door on the left and returned a couple of minutes later with a large forest green sweater and some gray sweatpants. He held them out to me, and I took them automatically.

"You need a bath." Dorian's voice was gentle. Like warm silk on my icy skin. "The door in the middle leads to a private bathroom. There's a towel already in there. You can put your clothes in the hamper in the corner. Clean up, relax, and then we'll talk."

I turned to him and was about to argue, but Dorian held up his hands in surrender. "I promise I'll tell you anything you want to know."

Satisfied I would get some answers eventually, I made my way to the bathroom. I locked the door behind me and exhaled slowly. Calling the area spacious was an understatement. It was the size of the entire communal bathroom, but instead of several shower stalls, this bathroom only had one very large claw-foot tub to the left. The wood paneling was the same color as everywhere else in the building, but the paint above it was a rich teal. The slate-gray tiles should have made the room feel small and dark, but the contrast of the white fixtures brought the entire room together.

I slipped out of my shirt and tossed it in the wicker hamper in the farthest corner. My jeans took some wiggling, but I eventually pried them off too. I looked at the blood dried into the denim and my mind flashed back to Bethany's eyes, so devoid of life. Bile rose in my throat, and I swallowed it back down as I tossed the jeans into the hamper as well.

I turned the faucet in the tub all the way to the left and plugged the drain. Soothing steam soon filled the room and fogged the mirror. Carefully stepping into the tub, I sank down into the almost scalding water. The heat soaked into my bones. I took several slow, deep breaths in and out, trying to calm my nerves and my muscles.

Bethany's face kept flashing in my mind, so I did what I had done for over four months at that point. I put the images in an imaginary safe and locked them away, never to be seen again. Arranged on a small table next to the tub sat several expensive brands of soaps and body wash. I took a random one and scrubbed off the blood that had seeped through my clothes. The water ran crimson, so I let the water out, refilled the tub, and scrubbed my entire body once more.

Feeling satisfied that I had gotten the gore off my body, I dressed in the oversized clothes Dorian let me borrow, and I padded back into the common room.

Dorian slouched on the couch, his arms resting on his thighs, and stared into the fireplace like he wanted to jump into the flames. I sank down beside him, and he didn't even glance at me. Instead, he sighed and closed his eyes.

"What happened to Bethany should have never happened," he started. "It was supposed to be a routine... then something went wrong, I'm not sure what, and they *improvised*. I tried to warn them not to. That it would bring consequences we wouldn't be able to foresee..." Dorian took a deep breath and stared intensely at me. "It got messy, and now you're involved... but maybe you've always been involved."

I swallowed before speaking. "You're talking about the shadowy thing that tried attacking us a few weeks ago."

Dorian paled. "You remember that?"

I squared my shoulders. "I remember everything."

Dorian jumped up from the couch, making me flinch, and started pacing. The flickering shadows the fire cast made him look ominous and otherworldly.

"Damn it, damn it, damn it!" he shouted. "You shouldn't be able to remember that, and if you can… damn it! I should have stopped him. But why you? It makes no sense. You aren't his normal type. You aren't particularly kind or shy, and you look nothing like my —"

He clamped his lips shut and pinched the bridge of his nose, exhaling.

I tried to interject and protest the fact that he just said I wasn't a kind person, but the words dried up. My eyes followed him as he continued to pace back and forth, rambling to himself. Who didn't I look like?

I sprang up and blocked his path. He glared down at me, his eyes blazing with such anger and intensity that I didn't dare breathe wrong. We stood like that for what seemed like forever, both of us just staring. His expression turned from anger to something else just as intense. The back of his hand caressed my cheek, and I leaned into that touch, letting go of the breath I definitely knew I had been holding. Dorian licked his lips and swallowed. His hand went from my cheek and cupped my chin, tilting my head up.

He leaned down, and our lips were mere centimeters apart. I wanted to close the distance between us, but his hand kept me firmly in place.

"Why you?" His whispered voice was strained, and it made me yearn for him even more.

"What do you mean?"

The door flung open, and Dorian yanked me behind him, and a sound I can only describe as a guttural growl erupted from his throat.

The two people who had entered the room stilled. Dorian was keeping me mostly out of sight, but I could see a flash of light brown hair from over his shoulder.

"Joel?" I asked.

He leaned to the side and peered over Dorian's shoulder.

"You look familiar. Have we slept together before?"

My top lip curled back. "No."

Joel shrugged and sauntered over to the pool table. The other boy had black hair and tawny brown skin. He was the other one I had seen with Dorian in the cafeteria. His eyes were different colors, one a bright blue, and the other a deep green, both narrowed, staring at me.

"What is she doing here, Dorian?" His voice was strained, and he had a slight Middle Eastern accent.

Dorian kept his body firmly in front of me. "That is none of your concern, Odion." His voice was deep and icy.

Odion didn't seem fazed by Dorian's bone chilling tone, but he shifted his eyes from me to Dorian.

"The headmaster won't like this," he said.

"Then don't tell him," Dorian suggested.

Odion took a step toward us, and Dorian's stance coiled.

Odion paused and put his hands in the air. "I'm on your side, just tell me what I can do to help."

"It's a little late for that," Dorian scoffed.

He grabbed my wrist roughly and started leading me toward the far left door.

"It doesn't matter what you do, Dor. He's going to get what he wants," Joel said.

A small yelp escaped my lips as Dorian halted and tightened his grip on me.

"What does that mean, Joel?"

I peeked over my shoulder, and Joel smirked as he lined up his pool cue with the triangular arrangement of multicolored balls.

"I know why the girl is here," he said, "with you. He's already claimed her, and you know it too, otherwise you wouldn't be acting like such a dick."

Dorian let go of my hand, and with speed I couldn't comprehend, he jerked Joel away from the billiard table and pinned him against the pane of the window. The glass cracked from the force and Joel laughed. Which was probably difficult to accomplish, considering Dorian's forearm was digging into his throat.

"Now you have to tell her, don't you?" Joel choked out.

Throughout the entire interaction, I didn't dare move. I only watched the interaction unfold in morbid fascination.

The window crunched as the panes splintered more, and Odion stalked over to Dorian, roughly clasping his shoulder.

"Enough," Odion said. "The last thing we need is another dead body. Even if Joel deserves your wrath right now."

Joel still smirked like nothing was wrong. Dorian let out one last growl and let him go. He turned to me, his silver eyes burning. Literally glowing with silver fire.

I gasped and covered my mouth. Dorian didn't move toward me, he just stood there, clenching and unclenching his fists.

After a moment, I spoke. "Wh-what are you?"

Dorian closed his eyes, visibly trying to get himself under control. When he opened them again, his eyes were their normal hue.

"He's a demon," Joel answered.

Dorian shot daggers at Joel, but he trudged over to the armchair closest to me and sagged into it. He said nothing, and that was all the confirmation I needed. My mouth was open for several seconds as I stared at each of them and then I burst out laughing. No one else joined in. My laughing slowly turned to hyperventilating, and the room felt too small. Too hot. The corners of my vision dimmed, and I remember Dorian rushing toward me with superhuman speed as I passed out.

Chapter Seven

THE DIM GLOW FROM a bedside lamp greeted me when I finally came to. I took in my surroundings and noticed that the room had a similar arrangement to mine but was vastly different. The walls weren't the navy blue I had grown accustomed to over the last couple of months, but a deep purple. The paneling was different as well, painted black instead of that rich reddish brown. I threw back the off-white sheets and was just about to get to my feet when someone softly knocked on the door.

The knob turned and Dorian poked his head in. I reclined against the stack of pillows as he trod carefully to the end of the bed. I pulled the duvet that was at the edge of the mattress over me, its black fabric like silk against my hands. Dorian cocked his head as he studied me. I wasn't going to talk to him. I didn't even know if I trusted him.

So I crossed my arms and stared at the duvet, watching the way my movements made the fabric shimmer. Dorian sighed, and my eyes betrayed me as they peeked up in time to see him sit down on the corner of the mattress, his eyes never looking away from me. I quickly cast my gaze back on the duvet.

"Ophelia?"

I didn't answer. He tried again.

"How are you feeling?"

I brought my arms closer to my chest and shrugged. "Fine."

Dorian groaned. I finally looked at him, and he seemed at war with himself.

"What's wrong?" I asked.

He huffed harshly. "Are you seriously asking me that? You shouldn't even know what I am, and yet here we are."

"Yes, here we are, because..."

Dorian shifted further onto the bed, and with a resigned sigh, he asked, "What do you want to know?"

His silver eyes glowed in the dim brightness, and I had the answer to my first question.

"You really aren't human." My voice was barely audible even to me, but he somehow heard it.

He ran his hand through his luscious brown locks and closed his eyes. When he opened them again, they were full of resolve.

"My mother was human. My father... well, my father's not. He's also a son of a bitch, but what else would you expect from a Divine Demon?"

My eyebrows knit together. "A what?"

Dorian squirmed. "Divine Demons are the highest born demons, besides the royal line, and they are extremely powerful, cruel, and dangerous."

"So, your dad is... a demon, and your mom is human, making you a half demon?"

Dorian huffed and glared out the window. "That's the nice way to put it. Half-breeds like us are called *Nezoras*. Nezoras don't belong. We're curses on the world. We're... wrong."

His eyes unfocused, like he was reliving a memory. A not-so-pleasant one by the way he shuddered, and when he focused on me again, the silver in his irises blazed.

"My father is a disgrace back in his realm. Banished to the earth realm by his own wife, but to him, it was the best thing that could have happened. Humans revered him and worshiped him as a god. He met my mother, he claimed her as *his*, and when she finally agreed, they had me. She died not long after."

I snatched a fistful of sheets as the memories I had tried so hard to keep at bay flashed through my mind. The silence after the scream, save for the intermittent sound of creaking rope. I took a slow, deep breath in and relaxed my hands as I exhaled, banishing the memory back to its imaginary safe.

"I'm sorry," I said. "Were you two close?"

Dorian flashed a ghost of a smile. "She passed when I was five, so I don't have many concrete memories of her, but I've always had this image of feeling warm. Like the rays of the sun shining just for me. What about you?"

My eyes widened slightly as I met his stare. "What do you mean?"

Dorian shifted his weight, so our knees brushed. It was a simple gesture, but the touch calmed me.

"You lost someone close to you, am I right? The way you reacted when I told you my mom died, it was like you knew the feeling."

His eyes bored into mine as my mouth opened, but no sound came out. My lips trembled, and I avoided his intense gaze.

"I don't want to talk about it," I said.

Heat rose to my cheeks as Dorian leaned forward and pressed his lips to my temple. He pulled back immediately.

I had never seen Dorian Whitmore sheepish. Arrogant and sarcastic, yes, but he never seemed embarrassed about anything. I smiled and leaned forward, my lips brushing against the sharpness of his jaw. Dorian turned his head slightly and the heat of his breath hit me full force. I wanted to lean in, but Dorian hesitated.

"Don't you want to kiss me?" I whispered.

Dorian hovered inches from me, biting his bottom lip before hurling himself off the bed entirely. I huffed as cool air filled the space where he had just been.

"Of course I want to," he said through gritted teeth, "but I can't. There's something else you should know. That shadow you saw a few weeks ago, that wasn't just a simple brush with death. If he wanted to kill you, he would have, but... he's claimed you instead, and my hands are now tied. Quite literally if he discovers I've touched you."

I flung the covers off me and bolted out of the enormous bed. I marched up to him and crossed my arms in what I hoped to be an intimidating pose. Judging from Dorian's guarded look, it was working.

"Joel said the same thing. What does that mean, he 'claimed' me? And why does this demon, who's probably like a bazillion years old, think he can do that? I'm not a prize you win at the state fair."

Dorian regarded me with utter seriousness. "His name is Dhazor. He's a Divine Demon, but he's more like a divine dick, and he's claimed you to be his wife."

I stood there, staring like Dorian had spontaneously grown another head, for a solid two minutes.

Dorian's expression grew concerned, and he took a step toward me. I held up my hand in a warding gesture.

"His *wife*? I think there are a few problems with that." I held up each finger as I counted. "One being no one asked me, two being I'm only sixteen, and three, which I think is the most important point, I don't want to!"

Dorian sighed. "I told you Divine Demons are extremely powerful. No one can say no to them. Well, no one refuses them and stays alive, that is."

I put my hands on my hips and tossed my hair behind my shoulder. "Then I'll be the first."

Dorian blinked. "Bubbles, I like your attitude, but I just said..."

I threw my arms into the air. "The one thing I hate is people telling me what I'm supposed to do with my life, so again, I'm saying no."

Dorian gazed at me, his eyes roaming over my body, and stopping to stare into my eyes.

"What is it?" I asked after a minute.

He licked his lips and looked at me with such desire, I thought I would melt. Closing the few feet of distance between us, Dorian grabbed the back of my head roughly, tilted my face up, and kissed me.

His lips were like fire and ice against mine, and I couldn't get any oxygen, but I didn't want any. I fisted my hands in his hair, pulling slightly. He groaned and tightened his hold on my head, while his other hand wrapped around my waist and jerked me closer. There was no space between our bodies, and yet it wasn't close enough. He pulled us backward until his back hit the wall with a thump. My hands pulled his hair again, and he flipped us so I was against the wall. His lips finally broke from mine, only to trail deep kisses down my cheek, my jaw, my throat. I ran my hands down his back, and he pulled his lips back to mine as his tongue explored my mouth.

A pounding broke us apart, and a muffled voice spoke from the other side.

"Hey you raging hormonal beasts," Joel said, "would you mind waiting until the dorm is empty to get freaky? We're trying to watch a movie out here!"

Dorian chuckled against my lips, and my face was so hot it felt like it would melt off. I couldn't take the intensity anymore, and stared at anything other than his burning gaze. A gentle finger lifted my chin, and Dorian's eyes were blazing as I ogled at him. He placed a tender kiss on my forehead.

"Don't mind him," Dorian whispered against my skin. "He's just pissy because he knows this is going to make matters more complicated."

"Because I'm claimed," I said.

"Yes."

"And Dhazor is dangerous."

"Extremely."

With some difficulty, I unwound myself from Dorian and wandered toward the window. It was dark outside. Almost pitch black, except for a few faint lampposts glowing around campus. It had to have been after midnight, and after the day I had, I should've been exhausted. Instead, my body jittered, and for the first time in months, I could envision a clear path ahead of me. My life, my *future* belonged to me, not some demon. I whirled back toward Dorian and tossed my hair over my shoulder.

"No one tells me what I can and can't do, so I guess we're just going to have to find a way to stop Dhazor."

I heard cackling from the other room. I strode to the door and opened it to find Joel bent at the waist, holding his stomach from laughing, all the while Dorian never took his eyes off me.

"Something funny, Weston?" I asked.

He nodded as he took a deep breath, trying to stop himself from cracking up again.

"A thing like you go up against a Divine Demon? That's the funniest thing I've ever heard."

I put a hand on my hip. "What do you know about him?"

Joel had straightened, and he had about six inches on me, so I had to look up at him to sneer.

He still had a smirk on his face when he said, "You're gonna be about as formidable against him as your friend was."

Bethany.

Grief was a funny thing. Throughout the entire conversation between me and Dorian, I hadn't forgotten about her death, but her absence hadn't been as consuming as it had been earlier in the day. And now that Joel had just taunted me with her murder, I was pissed. I drew back my arm as far as I could and punched him in the gut with so much force he dropped to his knees. The sound that came from his lungs wasn't laughter.

Dorian chuckled as he walked up to me and threw his arm around my shoulders.

"I can't say that wasn't entertaining."

Joel shakily got to his feet, and I was about to throw another punch, but Dorian stopped me.

"Now, now, let's leave his dignity somewhat intact." He guided me around Joel, and toward the couch where Odion sat watching our exchange.

I hadn't even noticed he was there, but he wore a contemplative expression as Dorian sat beside him. I sat in the armchair to the left of the couch and didn't even look behind me as Joel stomped off to his room.

"You know," Dorian said to Odion, "you'll wrinkle prematurely if you keep scrunching your face like that."

Odion didn't stop scrunching his face.

Instead, he propped his head on his hand, which was fixed on the arm of the couch. "You know, we have to tell her about the other thing now."

Other thing?

"Not tonight." Dorian crossed one leg over the other and tilted his head back. "I don't want to overwhelm her."

I scrunched my nose. "Do I get a say in that?"

Dorian smiled slightly and glanced over at me. "Bubbles, it's been a long day for both of us, and you look like you're going to pass out on me again."

"I feel fine," I said.

Dorian arched an eyebrow, and his eyes brightened slightly as he regarded me. He was right. I probably looked like the walking dead, and as much as I wanted to stay awake to get more information, my eyes felt heavy and started drooping. I fought to stay awake, but the day's events must have caught up to me. With a yawn, I leaned my head back in the chair and fell asleep.

Chapter Eight

I DIDN'T REMEMBER DORIAN taking me back to my dorm, but I jolted upright as I woke up in bed. As I focused on my surroundings, however, I realized this wasn't my bedroom. The wallpaper was a golden butterscotch instead of the navy I had grown accustomed to, and the bed wasn't nearly as comfortable.

There was a knock on the door, and Alisa didn't even wait for an answer as she bounded in and looked appalled that I wasn't up and around yet.

"Why do I need to be dressed? And whose dorm are we in?" I asked as I rubbed my eyes.

She licked her lips and shuffled her feet on the tan carpet. "Faculty moved us to a different floor since... since our room is a crime scene."

Oh.

Alisa smiled, but I could tell it took effort for her to change the subject. "To answer your first question, you need to get dressed because the headmaster called an emergency assembly. Didn't you get the alert?"

My face scrunched. Alert? Oh crap.

"I can't get school alerts," I groaned. "My phone is in pieces and those pieces are currently being stored in an evidence locker."

Alisa shrugged. "Bummer, but you need to get dressed and get your ass down to the auditorium. Headmaster Keswick does not mess around with tardiness."

She left the room, and I groaned again as I threw off the covers. My feet hit the floor and heat rose to my cheeks. I was still in Dorian's clothes. I pulled them off rapidly, pausing slightly when the scent of fresh wood and musk hit my nostrils, and changed into my school uniform.

Students packed the auditorium and there was hardly any space to maneuver. I quickly found an empty seat in the back, next to a girl leaning forward in her wheelchair. She seemed enamored with the person who was speaking, and looking toward the stage, I could see why. The cadence of his voice was mesmerizing. And his face... My eyes bulged. That was the man in the portrait above our fireplace! No, that couldn't be right. This must be that man's great-grandson Alisa mentioned. He looked... familiar, though. Like I had seen him before. Then it hit me. The man I saw talking on stage was the same man who had caught me and Dorian by the library a few nights ago. His thin and dull hair was now full and shiny, and jet black instead of pale gray. His face had filled out and his complexion was deeper. And his eyes were no longer milky, either, but a brilliant hazel full of faceted color, and also staring directly at me.

I couldn't break away from his gaze. It was almost as if I were in a trance. The words he spoke sounded muffled, as if I was hearing him through earplugs, and the rest of the auditorium disappeared. It was just me and him, and his brilliant shimmering eyes.

A sharp pain broke through, and I winced as the auditorium and the chattering of the entire student body came back into focus. Dorian was sitting right beside me and had my hand in his. I glanced down and his thumbnail dug into my palm, piercing the skin. I jerked my hand away, and a small well of crimson bubbled up. The bastard made me bleed. I huffed as I turned my attention back to the stage where the headmaster was no longer solely focused on me but was still addressing the audience, and my breathing stopped.

"The death of a classmate is never easy," Headmaster Keswick said. "Bethany Woods was a kindhearted soul, as most of you have come to know over the last few weeks, and someone cut her life all too short yesterday. Today will be a day of remembrance and grieving, but tomorrow we will move forward. And as such, I am not only canceling classes for the day, but this evening there will be a public memorial service in the courtyard. Take your time and mourn this loss. Counseling will be available for those who need it. Thank you."

The auditorium erupted in applause. Dorian nudged me and I exhaled sharply. Teachers dismissed the student body, and the girl in the wheelchair regarded me curiously as Dorian and I stood to leave. I didn't look at her as we made our way out into the main hall, but something about her stare made me uneasy.

Students milled about, filling the room with echoes. It was almost overwhelming. Dorian was focusing on our surroundings as he interlaced our fingers, and I focused on the feeling of his warm skin on mine. The sensation was enough for me to concentrate on blocking out all the chatter, and I could relax a little. We made our way to the stairs, dodging people as we went. I looked behind me, and didn't notice the solid mass of someone until I bumped into them.

Dorian jerked me back against him, and I yelped at the movement as I looked up into the face of Headmaster Keswick.

"Mr. Whitmore, Miss Allan. It's good to see you two again." The headmaster's eyes drifted to our hands still intertwined and narrowed slightly. His expression was full of... rage? Jealousy?

I couldn't tell, but the next time he spoke, his voice was like ice. "I think the three of us need to have a discussion about PDA. My office. Now."

We made our way through the crowd, with a bunch of the students falling silent and watching us. Dorian took the attention in stride, walking with a swagger. I, on the other hand, shrunk into myself, not wanting any more eyes on me.

The trip was short, but felt like an eternity, and when the headmaster finally shut the door to his office, I slumped in relief. Dorian did not. As soon as the latch on the door clicked shut, his body stiffened like we were in danger.

The headmaster gracefully sat down in his high-backed leather chair and folded his hands together.

"Take a seat, you two." His voice was nails on a chalkboard.

Dorian tightened his grasp but dropped my hand a moment later. I sat in the chair to the right of the large mahogany desk, and Dorian sat in the chair to the left. His body never relaxed, and his eyes never left the headmaster's. I was about to ask why he was so uncomfortable when the headmaster directed a question toward me.

"So, Ophelia." He said my name slowly, like he was testing how it sounded. "How are you liking Raven's Cove Academy so far?"

I licked my dry lips and directed my attention toward him.

"I'm not sure," I said. "I guess I like it. Other than the... obvious."

Headmaster Keswick nodded. "Yes, your friend, Bethany. I was very sorry to hear of her passing —"

Dorian cut him off with a snort.

"And you, Mr. Whitmore" — the headmaster turned his head slightly — "This is your third year here, and I see you've already found some... extracurricular activities to keep yourself busy."

Dorian straightened his back, which was a feat considering it was already so straight I thought it would snap.

"My extracurriculars are none of your business," Dorian snarled.

The headmaster merely leaned back and smiled. "Of course they are. This is a prestigious academy, after all, and it is my duty to make sure every student is well cared for."

Dorian arched an eyebrow. "Is that what you told Bethany Woods's parents when she first came here?"

The headmaster's smile evaporated, and his eyes burned with actual flames, but before I could wrap my head around whether what I saw was real or not, the heat vanished.

Headmaster Keswick turned his full attention to me.

"Ophelia, when I saw your file come across my desk this summer, I was eager to welcome you to this academy. You are a very well-rounded individual, and your grades are immaculate. Even after what happened with..." He paused for a minute, and his gaze darted to Dorian. "Anyway, I must warn you that being friends with Mr. Whitmore here is not the smartest thing to do if you wish to succeed here."

Dorian outright laughed. "You're telling her to stay away from me? When it's you who isn't safe? That's a damn joke."

The headmaster ignored Dorian's outburst and continued. "If I may be so bold, Ophelia, I feel like a more academically inclined and capable partner would better nurture your natural talents here at the academy."

My mouth gaped. I couldn't believe the headmaster of my school was sticking his nose in my dating life. "I-I'm sorry, Headmaster Keswick, but I really don't think that's any of your business."

Headmaster Keswick rubbed his chin. "That may be so. But think about what I've said. My only goal is for you to succeed at this academy. Now" — he glanced at the clock on the wall — "this chat was fun, but I must make preparations for Bethany's memorial service. You two should go back to your respective dorms."

With that obvious dismissal, Dorian and I rose. I opened the door, but Dorian didn't move. He was just glaring the headmaster down, and Headmaster Keswick was staring back, smirking. I tugged on Dorian's sleeve and he slowly backed away, following me out of the room.

Dorian's whole body was shaking as I steered him up the stairs that led to the dorms. It was a fight to get him to the first landing. He kept turning and descending a few steps until I grasped his arm to stop him. When we finally got to the second floor,

Dorian seemed to relax ever so slightly. He still had his hands balled into fists, but his shoulders didn't look so rigid.

The door to his dorm room was ajar, and I made my way to open it, but Dorian whirled me toward him and kissed me. I melted into his touch, but his lips felt off. Our kiss last night was soft and full of passion. This kiss felt hard and possessive. I broke the kiss, and the look in Dorian's eyes was wild.

"What's going on, Dorian?" I caressed his cheek, and he closed his eyes.

When he opened them again, I could see rage in his expression but also defeat. He kissed my forehead, letting his lips linger there for a moment.

"Everything will be okay," he said, "I promise. For now, though, go back to your dorm and get ready for tonight. I'll come find you in the courtyard."

Dorian entered his room and shut the door behind him, and I trudged back to my own dorm in a daze. What was going on? Why did Dorian seem so angry? I didn't even notice when I walked into the common area and Rachel was lounging on the couch until she spoke.

"You look like death. Oh, well, I guess that was your friend, huh?"

That broke me out of my stupor, and I rushed toward her.

"How dare you!" I shrieked, "Bethany died less than twenty-four hours ago and you're making jokes? What the hell is wrong with you?"

Rachel held up her hands in defeat, but her face was smug. "All I was saying is that you look awful. Jeez, with that short fuse, I'm surprised you haven't been locked up by now. Especially with what happened this past summer."

I felt the color drain from my face. Every sarcastic remark I had sitting in the back of my head vanished.

"Wh- what?"

Rachel smirked at me. "I read your file, you know. Poor Ophelia, you've had it so hard. Everyone in your life seems to die when you're around. Coincidence? Maybe. You want to know what I think, though?"

Rachel paused. I couldn't answer. She swung her legs off the cushions and pranced up to me. Her breath was barely a whisper as she looked directly into my eyes and spoke.

"I think it's your fault he died, and I think it's your fault Bethany died. You're a curse," she said.

"Enough."

Rachel twirled toward Alisa, who leaned against the doorframe with her arms crossed. She was wearing a black fitted dress that had no business being worn to a memorial service.

"I was just making conversation." Rachel pouted.

Alisa raised a perfectly manicured eyebrow. "Really? Because she looks whiter than she did yesterday, and you made her cry."

My hand automatically went to my cheek, and sure enough, a single teardrop came away on the tip of my finger. I pushed past Rachel, shoving her out of my way as I ran to my room and slammed the door.

Alisa knocked softly and gingerly opened the door.

"Ophelia?"

I had to strain to hear Alisa's voice. I buried my face in my pillow and ignored her.

She sighed, and I heard footsteps, followed by another door opening. Rustling rang through my ears in the otherwise silent room, and I peeked to see what Alisa was doing.

I sat up on the bed and curled my knees to my chest as Alisa shuffled through my clothes, making faces at various articles.

"You don't have to do that." I sniffled.

Alisa turned toward me and smiled as she laid out a black pleated skirt and a black blouse. The shades didn't match exactly, though. The skirt was more of a deep black and the blouse had more blue tones in it. Alisa sat down beside me and bit her lip. It looked like she wanted to say something. I raised an eyebrow and told her to spit it out.

"I'm sorry about Bethany," she said. "I know I act like a bitch sometimes, but I really cared about her."

I tightened my grip on myself. "I'm sorry too. How are you dealing with it?"

Alisa shrugged. "I don't really know. I just feel sort of... numb. It doesn't feel real, honestly. It feels like she's going to walk through the door with another big stack of those nerdy books."

A ghost of a smile came to my lips. Alisa wrapped an arm around me and squeezed.

"Okay." She hopped off the bed and threw the clothes she picked out at my face. "Enough moping. Get dressed and let's party enough for all three of us."

I grabbed the outfit and threw Alisa a wide grin. She left my room and as soon as the door shut, my smile vanished. It wasn't like her to be so... nice. However, with Beth's death, maybe she was rethinking her life choices. I doubted it, but the thoughts vanished as I got ready for my best friend's impromptu funeral.

Chapter Nine

THE COURTYARD HAD TRANSFORMED into a candlelit oasis with hundreds of flames flickering from white wax pillars placed all over. On the ground, around the fountain, and in everyone's hands. And there were so many people. It seemed like the whole town had turned out for the memorial. How had word gotten out so fast?

I didn't have time to ask anyone because standing by the fountain, looking gorgeous in a solid black suit, was Dorian. He was examining the water with intense fascination, and I strolled up to him as silently as I could, so as not to disturb him. He didn't acknowledge me when I stood at his side. His hair was messy, like he had been running his hands through it over and over. I put a hand on his upper arm, and the only thing that told me he knew I was there was the light pressure of him leaning into my touch.

My attention turned to the fountain, wanting to know what intrigued him so much, but all I saw was the reflection of the fire and the vague shimmery forms of our bodies.

"Fire and water." Dorian murmured so quietly it was almost impossible to hear him over the chatter of the growing crowd. "Both are destructive on their own, and yet, together, they're balanced."

He pivoted toward me so fast I instinctively took a step away from him. His silver eyes burned bright in the dark, wild and dangerous, but also a beacon guiding me home. A thrill went through me at the thought. I had never felt such an intense attraction to anyone before.

"Just like we balance each other," he continued. "We're meant to be together, Ophelia."

Dorian's hands lashed forward and gripped my upper arms. I winced, and tried to get distance from him, but his fingernails dug in so hard I thought they would break skin.

"Dorian," I said, "stop. You're hurting me."

He laughed once. "Pain, pleasure. They're the same thing, really."

"No." I winced as his nails dug in deeper, and I vaguely wondered why no one was bothering to intervene.

Odion answered my prayers seconds later when he strode over to us and wrenched Dorian back. His nails didn't loosen, and the result was me being yanked with him. Odion still had his hand on Dorian's shoulder and stepped closer to him, whispering in his ear.

"Don't make me use this, man," he said. "I know Keswick has you upset, but that isn't her fault. Let her go."

My eyebrows knit together until a glint caught my attention from the corner of my eye. I looked down and resisted gasping out loud. A small knife was being pointed discreetly into Dorian's side, and the flame of a candle made the silver metal of the blade flash.

"You don't have the guts," Dorian growled.

Before Dorian could utter another syllable, Odion brought his arm back slightly and snaked it forward, plunging the knife into Dorian's torso.

Dorian grunted, and his hold loosened enough for me to wiggle out of his grasp.

The blade squelched as Odion plucked it out of Dorian's flesh and wiped both sides of the blade on his jeans while Dorian went to his knees, clutching his side.

"You should go, Ophelia," Odion said. "Enjoy the service."

I choked out a laugh. "What the hell just happened?"

"He said leave."

I whirled around to find several people standing in front of me. There were five people in total. Three girls and two boys. The boys looked almost happy to see Dorian bleeding on the ground.

"Did you not hear me? Leave," the girl in the middle said.

She had jet-black curly hair, and green eyes the color of uncut peridot. She was absolutely gorgeous, even with the gigantic sneer on her face. I didn't think I *could* move. I turned back to Dorian, who was still on the ground. His eyes were so wide the whites of them were showing. No, his eyes weren't white. They were molten silver. I started shaking. What was happening? I faced the group of people again and shrieked. One guy from the back of the group now towered over me. He was at least six inches taller than I was, so he had to lean over me, which made him more menacing.

"Go. Now. Or you won't be alive in the morning to be sorry," he said.

Taking a small step backward, I turned away from the scene and fled.

My feet raced until the flickering lights from the candles dimmed into the distance, and when I could no longer hear the voices of the crowd, I stopped and rested my hands on my knees. Once my breath returned to a normal pace, I took in my surroundings. I was at the far edge of campus on the complete opposite side of the courtyard.

Shit. I had no idea what time it was, but the memorial must have been starting soon. A thick line of trees curved in front of me, and a rundown glass building nature had reclaimed was nestled to my left. The only light around was from a lamppost that illuminated the sidewalk, and I inhaled the scent of the earthy air deeply. If I just followed the curve of the concrete, I'd find my way back to the courtyard. Eventually.

My feet thumped on the even surface, and I only stopped when I heard an extra set of footsteps walking in tune with mine. I pivoted, and a shock went through my body as Detective Russo stood motionless behind me, his large hands stuffed into his pockets. He didn't have a suit on, so I was pretty sure he wasn't on the clock. What was he doing here?

He pulled his hands out of his pockets and held them up as if trying to say he wasn't a danger to me.

"Sorry," he said, "I didn't mean to startle you, but I saw you running like you were being chased and got worried."

I huffed out a laugh. "Worried? You interrogated me for my best friend's murder yesterday. Why would you be worried about me?"

Detective Russo raised an eyebrow and strode toward me. "Who said I was worried about you?"

I gritted my teeth. "For the hundredth time, I didn't murder Bethany."

"For someone who didn't murder anyone, you're pretty defensive about it."

I crossed my arms and tossed my wind-tousled hair over my shoulder. "Wouldn't you be if you were in my position?"

Detective Russo pursed his lips. He still looked put together, even without the suit and tie. He wore a freshly pressed white button-down shirt and khaki slacks. Was he attending the memorial?

"Maybe," he finally said, and my heart skipped a beat, thinking he had answered the question in my head.

I drew my arms closer to my chest. "Then will you stop accusing me?"

He stuffed his hands in his pockets again, a move that was both graceful and intimidating.

"No."

I flung my arms into the air. "Why the hell not?"

His eyes shot behind me, and when he refocused on my face, there was an expression I couldn't name lurking beyond the surface.

"Because, Miss Allan, there's something sinister that's been going on in this town for decades, maybe longer, and this academy seems to be at the center of whatever that is. The fact of the matter is, the only evidence we have of Bethany's murder links back to you. Maybe you're innocent in your friend's death, maybe not. It's my job to find that out, but it's also my personal mission to uncover this town's secrets. And from what I've witnessed, there's no shortage of them."

A strong wind whooshed around us, rustling the leaves and making me shiver. It only lasted for a moment, but when the breeze died down, Headmaster Keswick stood a few feet from me and Detective Russo.

"Hello," Headmaster Keswick stretched out his hand toward the detective. "I don't believe we've had the pleasure of meeting. I'm the headmaster of Raven's Cove Academy, Mathias Keswick. And you are?"

Detective Russo seemed hesitant but clasped the headmaster's hand. "Detective Zachary Russo. I'm in charge of the Bethany Woods murder case."

"Ah, yes. Her death was extremely unfortunate, and the students and faculty will mourn her for quite a while," Headmaster Keswick said, "but I'm so relieved to hear her case is in the capable hands of the Ashton PD."

"Thank you," Detective Russo said. "Can I have my hand back?"

Headmaster Keswick let his hand fall to his side, but he stared at the detective as if he was contemplating the best place to dispose of his body.

"Now that introductions are over, I believe Miss Allan and I have a memorial service to get back to. You're welcome to attend if you're finished harassing my students."

Headmaster Keswick reached out his hand toward me, signaling me to follow him, and we strolled back toward the courtyard.

The headmaster and I walked in silence, the thumping of our shoes on the sidewalk the only sound in the night.

"Ophelia," the headmaster said, "if that detective bothers you again, let me know straight away."

My voice cracked. "He thinks I killed Bethany."

Headmaster Keswick paused in his steps, and turned so we were face to face. His hands were gentle on my shoulders, but his face filled with undiluted rage.

He schooled his expression into one of neutrality and squatted so we were on the same level.

"He's mistaken." The headmaster's voice was steady and full of conviction. "You are not her killer."

"How would you know that?"

Headmaster Keswick's lips curled at the corners, though it didn't meet his eyes. "Because I've read your file from your previous school, and nowhere in it mentions any anger problems or acting out. Especially after what happened to you this past summer." The mention of the incident made me flinch. "You're wholly good," he continued, "And I — I mean this school — needs someone like you."

I smiled. "Thank you, Headmaster."

"You're welcome. Now, let's go celebrate your friend's life."

He straightened, and we trekked back to the courtyard where everyone had gathered around the fountain Dorian and I were at earlier. I scanned the crowd for any sign of him or Odion, or even the group of people who had intervened, but none of them were anywhere to be found. My mouth turned downward as I found an empty spot next to an elderly couple. The man was using a walker, and he looked like he was going to collapse soon.

I cleared a couple of candles off the fountain's edge and called the man and his wife over to have a seat. They voiced their gratitude, and I turned my attention back to the campus steps as feedback from a microphone sounded.

Headmaster Keswick waited for a moment while people quit chattering.

"Bethany Woods was not only an exceptional student," he started, "acing every assignment given, but she was also an extraordinary human being. Tonight is not about mourning her death but celebrating her life. It's okay to grieve for the hole she has left in each of us, and that's why I've asked several students to come up here and share their stories about this amazing young woman who left us too soon."

Headmaster Keswick stepped aside as Joel stepped over and adjusted the microphone. My jaw clenched. I didn't hear a word he was speaking, because words shouldn't have even been coming out of his mouth. He had no right to speak about Bethany after what I overheard in the bathroom, which admittedly, I still wasn't sure what that was about.

I was about to march up there and demand answers when someone caught my attention. To my right, Bethany's parents were holding candles and listening to Joel's speech. Bethany's mom was sobbing into her husband's chest, and her dad looked... empty. And suddenly, whatever Joel was saying didn't matter. These two people who had just lost their daughter were the only ones who mattered right now. I made my way over to them. Bethany's dad saw me approaching first, and his face no longer looked empty. He was furious.

"How dare you show your face here," he said. "You have no right to be at this memorial after what you did."

Bethany's mom uncovered her face at the sound of her husband's yelling and made a tiny gasping sound when she saw me. She disentangled herself from her husband's arms and strode toward me. I was having a hard time breathing. I was expecting her to slap me or spit on me, but she just stared.

Her eyes were the same shade as Bethany's, and her nose was the same shape. It almost felt like I was looking at my best friend again.

"I just want to know why," she said, "why kill my little girl?"

I opened and closed my mouth several times, and no sound came out.

"Tell me why you killed her!" she screeched.

Joel stopped mid-sentence. In fact, the entire crowd had gone silent and was now gawking at the confrontation happening in the middle of them.

"I-I didn't..."

I could feel the space closing in around me. My lungs felt like they were being filled with cement, and my vision was going black around the edges. I had to get out of there, and this time, I needed away from the entire school.

So I bolted.

Chapter Ten

THE DESERTED, MOONLIT STREETS of Ashton surrounded me. Everyone was, presumably, at the memorial service, and the only signs of life were flicking streetlights and the occasional resident that wasn't at the school, walking their dog. The New England autumn air bit at my skin through the thin fabric of my blouse until I had to wrap my arms around myself to keep warm, but it did little to help. My heart rate had slowed a while ago, but I still kept count of my breathing.

In one, two, three, four.

Hold one, two, three, four.

Out one, two, three, four..

I was concentrating so much on counting that I lost track of where I was going until I observed the world around me and realized I had no idea what part of town I was in. Buildings that looked at least a hundred years old surrounded me, and I found a pathway that wound between the worn, red brick structures. As I wandered aimlessly up the uneven cobblestone path, I couldn't help but wonder if people of the past walked on the same stones, and how they felt traipsing through the dark.

A figure hidden in shadow emerged from a dark alcove, and before I could fill my lungs to scream, he clamped his hand over my mouth and shoved my back against the bricks.

"Shh. It's only me."

I took his hand away from my mouth and wrapped m arms around his neck. "Dorian, you're okay!"

He embraced me back fiercely and nuzzled his face in the crook of my neck.

"I'm okay," he assured me.

We broke the embrace, and Dorian smoothed my hair. "I heard about what happened at the memorial. How are you doing?"

His voice was as gentle as his hands smoothing my hair, and something inside me broke. My knees could no longer hold me up, and Dorian bore my weight as we sank to the uneven, hard surface of the cobblestone road. My body shook violently as sobs overtook me.

Dorian pulled me into his lap, rocking us back and forth. His hand still smoothed my hair down while his free arm wrapped tightly around my waist. I cried and cried until I started coughing, and even then, the waterfall of tears didn't stop.

I didn't know how long we sat there in the cold like that, but eventually, the tears stopped, and I could think more clearly.

I looked into Dorian's eyes. They were glowing softly, like the light cast down from the moon, bathing everything in a blanket of calm. There was no sign of the earlier turmoil, and while acting like that was never acceptable, I let it slide for the night, considering everything that had happened.

Instead, I grabbed his face between my hands, which was a feat considering how entwined we were, and brought his lips down to mine. This kiss was gentler than our first, but every bit as passionate. Dorian tightened his hold on me, tangling his fingers in my hair, tugging at the strands slightly. I gasped into his mouth, and he moaned. I moved my hands from his face to his hair, and mirrored the action, pulling gently. He moaned again and grabbed my bottom lip between his teeth.

I inhaled like I couldn't get enough air, and only he could give me the oxygen I needed to live.

He broke the kiss first, panting, and laid his forehead against mine as we both tried to catch our breath. Dorian kissed my forehead and moved me from of his lap once we both calmed down. He helped me off the ground, and the cool night air once again enveloped us.

Dorian laced his fingers through mine and pulled me down the road. "Come on, I want to show you something."

His tone suggested that whatever he needed me to see was serious, so I made no arguments as he led me to the center of town.

I bounced on the balls of my feet to warm myself as Dorian picked the lock to the local library.

"Aha!" he yelled as he opened the heavy glass door.

We strolled inside, and Dorian flipped on the lights. The library wasn't big by any means, and it certainly wasn't as big as Raven Cove's, but shelves stacked high with books filled the space. How could people write so much? I peered at Dorian, who was regarding me curiously.

"Why bring me here?" I asked.

Dorian cleared his throat and shuffled his weight from one foot to the other. Was he nervous?

"There's a collection of books here I want you to see." His voice was barely above a whisper.

He trudged ahead, and we walked until we stood in front of an aged, ornately decorated door. It looked heavy, like one of those doors you might see in a castle. *Or at Raven's Cove Academy*, I thought.

Dorian took a thick iron key from his pocket and turned the lock until there was a chunky click. He pulled the handle, revealing a set of stone stairs that we carefully maneuvered with help from his phone's flashlight. The room at the bottom was more of a basement filled with even more books than upstairs. Some looked new, maybe published within the last twenty or thirty years, but a lot of them looked ancient. Hues of brown and green leather-bound tomes of varying heights, all with golden lettering on the spines, were in various positions across the shelves. One such book instantly caught my eye, and I meandered toward it, ignoring Dorian calling after me to be careful.

My arm extended toward the book, and a fizzle of static shock bit my fingers as soon as they grazed the binding. Picking up the book, I carried it over to the only table, a wide, solid piece of wood that looked like it had been a piece of a ship or a building that hadn't been able to withstand the test of time. The chair wobbled as I sat down. Dorian lit the candelabra in the center with a long match and took a seat beside me. My heart picked up speed, and I didn't understand why. I had never seen this book before, but something about it seemed familiar.

There was a symbol on the cover that looked like a giant X with arms, two golden dots on the top and bottom, and a line slashing through the center. An embossed Latin phrase curved over the symbol, and it read:

Divinus Daemonis Magia Compendium

"Compendium. Like a collection of things, right?" I ran my fingers over the soft, worn leather. It seemed like someone had handled this book hundreds, maybe thousands, of times.

Dorian bit his lip before answering. "The Divine Demon's Magic Compendium. Out of all the books in here, that was the one I was really hoping you wouldn't pick up."

"What is it?" I flipped open the heavy cover. The pages were thick and aged, their edges ripped in places.

"It's a spell book," Dorian explained, "for Divine Demons. It houses all their most powerful and dangerous rituals."

My fingers paused as I looked up at him. "Like your dad?"

Dorian ran his hands through his hair. "Exactly like my dad."

I thumbed through several pages, each one more confusing than the last, until my eyes skimmed over the word *mortem*. I looked at the large, elegantly penned letters closer.

"What's this one?" I asked Dorian.

"*Mortem Revocare*. Translated, it means 'Reverse Death,' and I know what you're thinking. The answer is no."

"I wasn't thinking anything." I lied.

Dorian scoffed. "Dead is dead. There's no changing that. Nothing good can come from that spell, or anything else in that evil book."

I rested my cheek on my fist in defeat. He was probably right. I flipped to the next page and my heart stopped. A portrait of a man stared at me. Not just any portrait either, but the same portrait of the founder of Raven's Cove Academy that hung above the fireplace in my dorm. Opposite that were scrawls of handwriting that looked like a list, and a folded-up piece of paper in the gutter of the pages. I plucked the loose sheet out of the book and read the scribbles across from the portrait. There were several names, each with a date and cause of death, except the last one. No dates of birth, or pictures, and with each name and date my eyes skimmed, the more it made sense why the current headmaster resembled the founder of Raven's Cove Academy so much.

Theodore Kenphrey — Died August 1895 — Suicide

Ansel Bellwood — Died September 1927 — Gunshot to the chest

Alexander Branton — Died January 1968 — Drowned

Wyatt Claynor — Died July 1998 — House fire

Mathias Keswick —

Headmaster Keswick wasn't related to the founder of the school, he *was* the founder, and he didn't seem to have aged a single day. I unfolded the paper between my fingers. It was another photo, but compared to the rest of the book, this picture was relatively new. A woman was in the center of the frame with a man standing behind her, his hands on her shoulders, and a sad-looking little boy who couldn't have been over four years old sat in her lap.

The man was Headmaster Keswick. I didn't recognize the woman beside him, though. She had flowing brown hair and green eyes that held empathy and kindness, and the boy... I gasped. The boy had a mop of dark brown hair a few shades darker than his mother's and silver eyes that seemed to glow even through the photo.

Dorian snatched the photo out of my hand.

"You weren't meant to see that," he said between clenched teeth.

I looked at him through a new lens. Everything clicked into place, and I faced Dorian. His skin was pale, and he clenched his fists so tightly they were shaking.

"You said your dad was a Divine Demon, but that's not the whole truth, is it?"

My eyes never left his as he slowly shook his head.

"Headmaster Keswick is a Divine Demon, and he's also your father."

Dorian lowered his chin in confirmation.

A chill ran down my spine as I put together another piece of the puzzle.

"Headmaster Keswick... your dad... is Dhazor."

Dorian bit his bottom lip but said nothing. It didn't even look like he was breathing. Slowly though, he nodded once more.

The room spun around me, and the walls felt way too close. Breathing became difficult. I could hear Dorian saying something, but his voice felt too far away for me to comprehend his words. I jumped out of my chair so suddenly it fell backward onto the concrete floor.

"I have to get out of here." I didn't even know if I said the words aloud, but Dorian seemed to understand, anyway.

He blew out the candles and led me through the exit, careful not to touch me. I was grateful for the gesture, but I honestly didn't know how to feel otherwise. As soon as the cool night breeze hit my face, I gulped in air and slowly, my surroundings steadied.

"I've wanted to tell you. About everything, but —"

I held up my hand in front of me, cutting Dorian's words off.

"Not tonight," I said. "I just... I just need some time to process all of this."

Dorian nodded. "I understand. Let's get you back to your room, then."

We walked back to Raven's Cove Academy in utter silence. We didn't even say anything to each other when we went to our respective dorms. I clicked my bedroom door shut well after curfew, and luckily, Alisa didn't seem to see me come in. My knees wobbled, and I didn't make it two steps before my body collapsed onto the soft carpet.

What the hell was happening, and why did it have to involve me? I couldn't wrap my head around the events of the last couple of days. Had it really only been two days since Bethany's death? No, that couldn't be right. I nestled my face into the tan-colored fibers and cried until I fell asleep.

Chapter Eleven

T HE GOLDEN HUE OF my walls was the only scenery I laid eyes on for the next several days. One of my teachers brought the nurse to my room after the third day of not going to class, and I gave a rather convincing performance of being sick. The nurse excused me from school for the next two days, or until she gave me a clean bill of health.

Or until Headma — Dhazor — comes up to my room and makes me go.

Dorian didn't come by to check on me at all in those days, and that was how I wanted it. I was done with him, and his messy hair, and sexy smile, and the way he smelled like fresh musky earth when he held me, and...

"Ugh!"

I yelled and smacked a pillow over my face in a vain attempt to keep the mental images at bay.

I still couldn't wrap my head around the chaos that was happening. I had been replaying everything that happened on repeat, trying to figure out what I missed, and every time my eyes closed, I saw Bethany's body, Dorian's burning eyes, the room under the library. Over and over until I could no longer stand it. I needed answers, and Bethany needed justice.

The pillow flopped onto the floor next to several piles of dirty clothes as I forced myself out of the warmth of my bed and rummaged through my clean wardrobe. Or what was left of it.

I pulled on a pair of slightly paint-spattered jeans and a stretched-out mustard-yellow tee shirt from the only year I went to summer camp. I flung open my bedroom door and grimaced as I glimpsed myself in the mirror. My hair looked like a tumbleweed. A big sandy-blond frizzy mess. Grabbing a hair tie from my dresser, I quickly threw my hair in a bun as I continued stomping out of the dorm. I was halfway down the last flight of stairs when I noticed Joel and Rachel snuggling in an alcove between lockers. I saw red as I threw my shoulders back and made a beeline toward them.

At least I had been until someone riding a bike knocked me to the ground. No, not a bike. I got to my feet and brushed myself off, and saw the tire of a wheelchair, and the straight midnight-black hair of the girl I sat next to in the emergency assembly.

"Come with me." Her voice was urgent, and she was peering around as if she were afraid someone was watching us.

I was too dumbfounded to say anything, and when I didn't move, she pushed her wheelchair into me.

"Move," she said, "before they spot us together."

That got me walking, and we weaved our way through the sea of teenagers trying to get to their next class, only stopping when we found a supply closet with the door ajar. We snuck in, and she closed the door behind us.

"What do you think you're doing?" The girl crossed her arms and looked at me expectantly.

"What do you mean?"

She gave me a look that said she wasn't messing around, and I huffed.

"I'm going to confront Joel and get some answers," I said. "By the way you stopped me just a second ago, though, I'm thinking you might be in on this whole 'demon' thing and can clear a few things up."

"Confront Joel?" The girl snickered. "And you think Joel will, what? Come right out and tell you everything, and you two will become best buddies and go skipping down the hallway arm in arm? Don't be ridiculous. You know nothing about what's going on."

"Then tell me!"

The girl grabbed the arms of her wheelchair. "No. The safest thing for you to do is to stay away from Dorian, come to terms with your friend being dead, and move on."

Tears were in my eyes, and the girl stared at me for a solid minute without blinking.

"Shit," she muttered.

She sucked on her teeth and started admiring her nails.

"Tomorrow, the Divine Order is meeting for All Hallow's Eve," she said. "If you were to, oh I don't know, crash said meeting at exactly midnight by going down to the basement and following a secret passageway behind the HVAC unit, you *might* get some of your answers. But you figured all that out on your own."

Understanding hit me. No one was telling me what was going on because no one *could* tell me. I smoothed down a wrinkle in my shirt and played along.

"Of course I figured it out, because I'm just that clever. And you didn't have any knowledge of the crashing of said meeting, because why would I tell anyone?"

The girl grinned and started turning her wheelchair to leave.

Before we went our separate ways, she whispered, "I hope you know what you're getting yourself into."

Me too.

I spent the next few hours planning and preparing my next moves. Demons had to be like vampires, right? So, I needed to get my hands on some holy water, stakes, and garlic. I wished I had my phone right then so I could actually look up that theory. Would the internet even have that sort of information? I didn't know, but I knew if an all-powerful demon ran the school, the library downstairs might have what I needed.

The smell of books filled my nostrils as I entered the library for the first time since Beth's death, and the memories of the two of us snickering at our table in the back came flooding in. I tried to shake them off as best as I could as I strolled down the non-fiction section, my eyes roaming over every book on every shelf. I went up and down the aisle three different times, and there wasn't a single book about demons. Or vampires, for that matter.

I was about to give up and head back to my room, but there was a tug in my gut telling me not to. Instead, I headed into town, planning to stop at the library there, but unlike the night of the memorial, people were out and about, and more importantly, shops were open.

I wandered down Main Street, peeking into the windows of the various shops to see if anything in them looked useful, when I came across a weird-looking vintage store and went inside.

The small shop was dimly lit, and the scent hit me hard. It smelled like when I went to church with my friend back in elementary school, and I recognized it as incense. This must have been the spiritual shop Alisa mentioned.

I moved deeper into the building and noticed small bundles of what looked like dried grass tied together, next to several shimmering crystals of various sizes and colors. Tapestries of the moon phases and abstract art hung on deep purple walls. I wandered around until I heard a noise coming from the back, and a short elderly man with wispy white hair emerged from behind a clanking beaded curtain.

"Hello Ophelia," the man said.

"Who are you, and how do you know my name?" I asked.

The man chuckled and then coughed. "My name is Ernest, and I know many things, but in this case, a very determined detective came in with your picture."

I rolled my eyes. "What did Detective Russo want?"

Ernest grabbed my hand. His fingers were like ice, and I had to stop myself from shivering as he led us through the beaded curtain into an even more dimly lit room with a single circular table in the middle and two chairs across from one another. Flames from black candles danced on every shelf, illuminating skulls of different shapes and sizes that hung on the pitch-black walls.

"He wanted to know about skin carving," he said. "He seemed like a very disturbed man. Anyway, that isn't what's important right now. What's important is you're here for some information, yes?"

My brows furrowed. "I — um — yes."

I wasn't sure what to say to that question because, in truth, I hadn't been planning on even entering the store, let alone getting answers from an elderly man who didn't know what was happening at the academy.

Ernest motioned for me to sit, and the scrape of the chair legs against the shop floor made my skin crawl. He sat in the opposite chair and placed his age-worn hands on the table, palm up. I placed my hands in his, and his grip was surprisingly strong despite his frail appearance. Ernest leaned his head back and took several deep breaths. The fire rose and fell with his breathing and the surrounding air cooled, though I saw no ventilation anywhere. When Ernest leveled his head at me again, his eyes were pure white.

Not like Dorian's, though. Ernest's eyes didn't burn. They were... empty. Hollower than a corpse. I tried to jerk my hands out of his grasp, but his grip tightened to the point of pain. I winced and Ernest's mouth opened, but a voice that wasn't his spoke.

"Ophelia Allan. A child. A mere *human*. You are so young to have seen so much death. And more tragedy is to follow in your wake. Ask your question, but know you may not like what comes of the answer."

I straightened my spine and pushed my shoulders back, even as my body trembled.

"What happened to Bethany?" My voice came out strong and even.

Ernest's mouth opened once more, and the smell of decay washed over me.

"The scale is being altered," he said. "Light and Dark are now at odds, and the war that should never be won has changed course. Your friend was the beginning of the end, and unless you can stop her acolytes from sacrificing three more innocent souls by the time nature brings new life, the earth shall split open and Darkness shall reign."

Ernest gasped and slumped forward as his grip loosened. I ripped my hands away, and they shook violently as I waited for Ernest to come to. My heart rate had slowed by the time he stirred, and I reached across the table, resting my hand on his arm, comforting him.

"It's okay. Just take your time," I said.

Ernest had a nasty bump on his forehead from where he had hit the table, but otherwise he looked fine. He smiled shakily at me.

"Did I doze off in the middle of our conversation? How rude of me. I apologize, but I'm afraid that means I'll have to close up the shop early." He patted my hand, which was still on his arm. "Never get old, dear."

I returned his smile halfheartedly and rose, helping Ernest up as well. We slowly made our way to the door, and he wished me well as the lock clicked behind me. What the hell was going on in this town?

I couldn't sit still at all the next day. And since the nurse said I still felt clammy this morning, she excused me from classes for another day. Not that I minded, because my focus was on everything else besides school. Pacing the floor of my room for the thousandth time, the plan for tonight ran through my mind over and over. I would go down the secret tunnel, and once the Order started their meeting, I would pop out like a secret agent and yell "Freeze!"

No, that wasn't a good plan. I would secretly record their meeting and post it on social media. That wouldn't work either since I didn't have a phone, and I was pretty sure even if I had my phone, I would be dead before I could post anything. I groaned and fell face first onto the bed. I had no idea what I was doing, and I wanted so desperately to talk to Bethany about all of this. Or my mom.

A lightbulb went on in my head. I mussed my hair even more than it was, which wasn't that hard, and I made my way down to the office, careful not to let the headmaster know I was there. The last thing I needed right now was a run-in with him. Ms. Crane looked up as I entered, and alarm spread over her features. I guess making myself look sicker than they already thought worked a little too well.

"I'm fine," I croaked. "But I had a question. Since my phone has been... confiscated, I was wondering if there was a way for me to call my mom. She's probably really worried about me, and to tell the truth, I'm getting a little homesick."

A gentle smile spread over Ms. Crane's features, and she motioned for me to come around to her side of the desk. I scooted a chair over as she pushed the corded landline over so I could better reach it.

"I need to check a few things. I'll be back in a few minutes," she said.

I nodded my thanks and dialed my mom's number as soon as the door to the office closed. The phone rang once. Twice.

"Hello?"

The sound of my mother's voice broke something inside me. I hadn't known how much I needed to hear her soothing tone until she spoke.

"Mom?" I sniffled.

"Ophelia, honey, what's wrong?" She sounded alarmed.

"I w-want to c-come home." The uncontrollable sobbing made my voice shake. "It's terrible here. M-my friend died, and the police think I did it, and there are so many secrets here, and I don't know what to do, or who to trust, or —"

I cut myself off because if I wasn't careful, she would think I was losing it. I took a shaky breath and continued.

"Mom, I think I need help."

There was silence on the other end.

"Mom?"

She sighed. "I know, sweetheart, and I think the best thing for you to do is stick it out at the academy. The investigation will continue, and they'll find who really killed your friend. You just need to cooperate fully with them and be patient."

My stomach sank to the floor. "You've spoken to the police?"

"Yes. As for everything else you're worrying about, I'll call around and see if there's a decent therapist in the area. I should have done that before sending you to Ashton, and I'm sorry, but I understand you're without a phone right now, too. I'll send you one of my old ones. It's nothing fancy, but it will do for now."

I rolled my eyes. "I'm not sure a therapist can help with this."

"You never know until you try," she said. "You didn't think you'd like your old therapist, remember, and you ended up loving her."

I knew I wouldn't win that argument, so I just said, "Thanks, Mom. I love you."

"I love you too, honey. Hang in there. It will all work out."

The line went dead, and I choked back more tears as I heard the door to the office open. I turned, expecting to see Ms. Crane only to find Headmaster Keswick, or rather, Dhazor, standing before me.

"Hello, Headmaster." I tried to keep my voice even.

He smiled, but it felt cold. "Hello, Ophelia. You look dreadful. Are you feeling alright?"

I licked my lips and tried to slow my heart rate. "I've been feeling sick this past week, but I'm on the mend."

The headmaster's smile curled a little more on one side. "I'll look forward to seeing you in class next week, then."

My lips turned down. "See me in class?"

The headmaster schooled his expression into one of neutrality. "I'm substituting your English class while your teacher takes care of a... family emergency."

My heart thrummed. His entire demeanor screamed danger, and I had to get away from him.

"I'm still feeling a little icky, honestly. I'm going to go back to bed."

I brushed past the headmaster and didn't relax until the heavy wood of my dorm door clicked behind me.

Chapter Twelve

I STARED AT THE ceiling for hours until the alarm on the bedside clock buzzed 11:00 pm. Taking a deep breath, I pushed off the covers and threw on the black pants and black turtleneck hanging over the back of the desk chair. Tying my hair in a loose ponytail, I took another slow, deep breath. I could do this.

Heavy bass and chatter filled my ears as I made my way down the stairs. Another dorm party, I supposed, and since it was Halloween, it made sense. Leaving the thumping music behind, I stepped onto the main floor. I knew the access to the basement was behind a door on the main floor, but the faculty kept which door a tight-lipped secret. I eyed the doors I knew led to classrooms. The rest were unmarked, so I did what any rational person would do.

I opened every door I came across.

Most of them were classrooms and supply closets, but there was one at the end of the hall tucked away in an alcove. A small block of weather-beaten, broken wood kept it cracked. I opened it to pitch blackness, but I could make out the first couple of concrete steps. I cursed myself for not bringing a flashlight. It was well past eleven-thirty, and I didn't have time to run back upstairs and grab anything. I wasn't even sure if there was a flashlight in the dorm, and once again I wished I had my phone with me. I would just have to be careful on my way down.

Stepping onto the first step, I shut the door as much as the wood block would allow and brushed my hand along the rough surface of the wall as I slowly descended into the basement. The roar of heavy machinery grew louder with each deliberate step I took.

My hand brushed against something jutting out from the wall, and feeling around, I noted it was a light switch. I turned it on, and some florescent lights overhead flickered to life.

The HVAC unit sat in the far right corner of the large room. It honestly looked more like a cave than a basement. The concrete floor met with brown rocky walls, and the air was thick and humid. I wandered over to the enormous piece of equipment, peered behind it, and groaned. There was no passageway. No secret door. Just a rocky surface.

I leaned my head against the wall and sighed. I didn't know what time it was, but I was pretty sure midnight had come and gone, and I was about to give up when a shiny drop on the floor caught my eye.

Squatting down, I saw the dim light reflect off a fresh drop of deep crimson blood. I noticed a few more drops on the surface of the wall and craned my neck upward to find an odd-looking shape faintly carved into the wall. The symbol looked like a pentagram with sun rays bursting from the outer ring. There was a spiral in the center of the pentagram that was darker than the rest of the carving. I stood up and examined it closer.

The stone appeared wet, as if someone took a damp cloth and wiped off the area. My eyebrows knit together as my gaze darted from the blood drop on the floor to the indentation on the wall and back and an idea popped into my head. I pressed my palm into the rough surface of the wall next to the symbol and dragged my hand down. I winced as the rocky texture dug into my skin, but my face fell as I realized my flesh was still intact, and I had nothing on me to cut myself with.

I frantically glanced around me, seeing if there was a stray piece of metal, or an exposed nail, but found nothing. I threw my head back and groaned in frustration. Midnight had to be min-utes away, if it hadn't already passed the hour, and I was no closer to getting into that meeting. It would've just been easier to gain an invitation into the Order.

The light glinted off the single drop of blood once more. Des-peration took over, and I dipped my pointer finger into the cool, tacky liquid. I smeared the blood over the center spiral and the symbol glowed an ominous red. I hadn't expected that to work, but the glowing light splintered outwards from the carving and wound its way into the rectangular outline of a door. The floor shuddered, and I stepped back as the red glow brightened until the entire room lit up. The red light died down as the door disintegrated, leaving a long passageway in its stead. I blinked a few times and forced my feet to move. The wall closed behind me, leaving me in darkness.

A few steps into the passageway and I gasped as torches on either side of me burst to life, and after the initial shock of fires lighting themselves, I jogged down the vast hall until I heard muted voices speaking — no, chanting — in unison.

I hunkered behind a corner that led to curved stairs made of the same warm stone as the walls. The words sounded foreign, but the air grew colder, and it became hard to get a breath in. It felt like a cinderblock had been placed on my chest. I snuck down the stairs as quietly as I could, which was difficult considering some steps were worn in certain areas, as if this staircase had been in constant use for centuries and each person's footsteps had eroded a small piece of stone.

My foot went to take the next step down, but I miscalculated the distance, and before I knew what was happening, I went tumbling. I collapsed onto more uneven stone, and I blinked rapidly, trying to reorient myself. When my vision finally cleared, several sets of eyes stared at me, including narrowed ones of burning silver.

The silence seemed to stretch for hours, even though it was probably more like half a minute, then someone to my right burst into laughter. I looked over and the girl in the wheelchair clamped a hand over her mouth, presumably to keep herself from laughing again. My eyes roamed to the others standing around the room. I counted eleven teenagers, but I didn't know who any of them were as they all wore maroon cloaks with the hoods drawn. I tried to stand, but pain shot through my leg and I ended up back on the ground. Putting my feet under me, I once more tried to stand. The pain was unbearable, and I would have fallen again if someone hadn't gripped my arm and held me upright. I glanced through my lashes to find Odion bearing most of my weight.

Once I thought I was stable enough, I tried to wriggle out of Odion's grasp, but his hand left my arm for a second before winding it around my waist. I noted Dorian in the far corner, glaring at the contact. He, too, wore a cloak, but his eyes glowed through the shadows. He hadn't moved an inch since I crashed into the room, but his eyes never left me. Odion must have clocked where I was looking because he chuckled.

"Looks like he's jealous." His whispered voice tickled my ear, and I felt my cheeks go hot.

Someone cleared their throat, and I looked over to find Alisa dropping her hood and stomping forward with her arms crossed tightly.

"What the hell are you doing here, Ophelia? Did you follow me?"

It would have been so easy to say yes, but I knew I had to play this right. I had to find out who killed my best friend, and the easiest way to do that was to play off what the girl in the wheelchair had told me and make these people think I was more clever than I actually was.

"No. I found this place by myself."

"How?"

The question came from one of the other people in the crowd. I glanced toward him and steeled my expression into one of neutrality. In reality, I wanted to freak out. The boy who had spoken was the one who threatened me the night of Bethany's memorial service. He had also taken his hood down, and I could see his features now that we weren't under the cover of nightfall. His hair was long and brunette, tied back into a short ponytail, and it looked like he regularly went to the salon and got highlights, which made his hair look more of a dark blond.

His eyes were shrewd, and I couldn't decide what color they were. In the flickering firelight that surrounded us, they looked green, then gold, then brown. He raised his eyebrows, and I realized he was still waiting for my answer.

"Uh, well, I, er, —"

"Having trouble speaking?"

Rachel's voice broke through the crowd as she also removed her hood and stepped forward. My stammering turned into a sneer. Odion tightened his grip on my waist. A warning. *Do not piss these people off*, he seemed to convey.

I once again willed my features to go neutral. "No trouble here. I found this place because, for a secret society, you all aren't that good at staying secret."

A few members who still had their hoods up scoffed. Rachel stalked closer and Odion tightened his grip on my waist to the point of pain as she stopped a few inches from my face. I didn't know what she was looking for, but whatever it was, she seemed to find it, and smiled cruelly.

"You're lying," she said. "You didn't find us on your own, but it doesn't matter, anyway."

Rachel whirled away from me, her hair smacking me in the face, and bounced into the middle of the group. My muscles tensed, and the only thing keeping me from ripping that perfect hair out was Odion's constant grasp restraining me.

"Looks like we found our new sacrifice, Dhazies." Her cruelty shone through her eyes, and I now had my prime suspect for Bethany's murder.

I looked at Dorian, whose face had paled, but still he said nothing. I couldn't help but be a little hurt that he hadn't come to my defense, but it was Alisa who spoke up.

"She can't be a sacrifice. It would look highly suspicious if both of my roommates ended up dead, and that would lead that nosy detective straight to us."

"You mean it would lead him straight to you?" One member spoke up. She stepped in front of Alisa and removed her hood.

She was beautiful. Like a fire goddess in the middle of her element. Her hair was bright copper that caught the flicker of the fire and made it seem like it was dancing alongside the flames, but her eyes were a cool blue, like water that was ready to douse the inferno if it got out of hand. Her frame was smaller than Alisa, but her demeanor made her seem taller than everyone in the room.

Alisa stood her ground, looking down at the girl. "That would be where he would start, Harper, but he would eventually find out about all of this," — she gestured around her — "and all of you."

"You're forgetting one thing, Alisa." Harper put her hand on her hips. "Sacrifices aren't supposed to die."

"Eventually they do," someone from the crowd said.

Harper whipped her head toward the voice. "Not helping, Gwen."

One of the still-hooded figures shrugged, and Harper sighed. "I'm outnumbered here, aren't I?"

Harper walked up to me and regarded me intently. "I'm sorry," she said. "Odion, bring her into the circle."

"No."

The voice came from behind me, and everything in my body tensed. That was the same voice I had heard in the courtyard all those weeks ago. Cold and ancient, slithering like a snake. Harper's eyes widened, and Odion froze beside me. Everyone else looked beyond me in both shock and awe. I wriggled out of Odion's grasp, and I turned to find Headmaster Keswick — Dhazor — standing on the stairs.

He took a few steps down, and everyone in the room, even Dorian, went onto one knee. Odion and I were the only ones still standing, and Dhazor seemed to find that amusing. He stepped down the rest of the way and took my chin between his fingers and smiled. I froze. It was like at the assembly when I couldn't look away from him.

"Odion," Dhazor said, "be a good boy and step away from my future bride."

Murmurs erupted. I broke his hold and glanced around. The only ones I could see who didn't look surprised at this revelation were Dorian and Odion.

"I won't ask again, boy," Dhazor said. "Slink back to the others or die where you stand."

Odion swallowed hard, but started moving backward, one step at a time. Dhazor rolled his eyes, and his jaw clenched. Before I knew what was happening, he flicked two fingers in the air and Odion flew into the far wall so hard, pieces of rock crumbled to the ground along with his unmoving body. No one dared make a move, or shriek in terror. I couldn't believe it. I ran to Odion's side and checked to see if he was still breathing.

"He's still alive." Dhazor sounded bored. As if he launches people into walls every day. And who knows? Maybe he did.

"He needs help," I choked out. "Someone help him."

Still, no one moved.

I tried to roll Odion over on his back, but moving the full weight of a person was harder than it seemed in the movies. I managed to roll him onto his side, and I gently lifted his head into my lap. Blood ran down the side of his face from a nasty gash, and I knew enough first aid to know that I needed to apply pressure. I slapped my hand over the wound and pressed down. The squelching must have gotten through to someone, because I heard footsteps rushing over and before I could utter a sound, Dorian knelt beside me and put his hands over mine, increasing the pressure.

Dhazor clicked his tongue. "Dorian, you've always been too soft."

I locked eyes with Dorian, and a thousand words seemed to be said all at once. I dipped my chin slightly, and Dorian removed his hands and launched himself at Dhazor.

Dhazor merely chuckled as Dorian hit an invisible wall. "Did you honestly believe you could challenge me? You're too weak, Dorian. You will never succeed me, you can't even match my strength."

Dorian hit the air over and over, but it was like a barrier of steel. Dhazor strolled further into the room, and everyone seemed to crawl backward in time with his steps. He smiled, and his eyes started glowing as red as the light that illuminated the passageway. Dorian shrieked in pain and plummeted to his knees. Blood seeped from his nose. I yelled at Dhazor to stop, but I couldn't move. Not while I was still trying to stop Odion's wound from bleeding.

Dorian's body relaxed as he slumped further into a heap on the ground. Dhazor knelt in front of him and whispered something I couldn't hear, then Dhazor's body turned into pure shadow, and he vanished.

Chapter Thirteen

O NCE DHAZOR DISAPPEARED, EVERYONE in the room
erupted into motion. A couple of hooded individuals
rushed over and took Odion out of my care, while Harper and
someone else still in a hood hurried over to help Dorian. I
was the only one who stayed where I was. It was like my veins
were full of quick-drying cement. I couldn't move, even when
Dorian was being half dragged up the stairs. Alisa and Rachel
were the only ones besides me who didn't seem to think any of
this was urgent. They stood in the corner and gossiped like it
was any other day.

The girl in the wheelchair rolled over and held out her hand.
I looked up at her as a few tears slipped down my cheek. I
hadn't even noticed I was crying. She peered at me with a mix
of sympathy and pity as I clasped her hand and pulled myself to
my feet.

"Let's get you cleaned up," she said. "My name is Willow Sasagawa, by the way. I don't think I've ever said."

I tried to smile, but it turned into a grimace, and if I hadn't still been holding Willow's hand, I think I would've collapsed.

"Nice to meet you, Willow." My throat felt raw.

Willow let go of my hand but had me roll her to the far back of the cavern where there was a well-concealed ramp that wound upward, and I was grateful that I had some leverage to keep myself upright.

"It goes back up to the basement," Willow explained.

I nodded and let my mind wander as we headed up the ramp and over to a service elevator that led to every floor of the school, including the dorms.

The echo of Dorian's scream reverberated through my mind. I felt useless. No, I hadn't just felt useless, I *was* useless. How was I supposed to go up against demons and magic? The answer was, I wasn't.

Willow led me to her dorm, and the common area looked nearly identical to mine. She guided me into the middle room and had me sit down on the pink floral bedspread to wait for her while she went to retrieve something. I did as I was told. I wasn't worried about staining the fabric, because if I got blood on the comforter, at least it would blend in with all the other various hues of red.

She came back a moment later with a sopping washcloth and handed it to me. I wiped my hands, red staining the fibers. There was nothing I could do about my pants, though. Luckily, they were black, so the blood was hard to see. Besides, they weren't the first pair of pants I had to toss because of blood stains. We didn't say a word to each other as I mindlessly kept cleaning my hands. I looked everywhere but at her. I didn't think I could take another stare full of pity. Instead, I focused on her room. How open and light it seemed compared to everything else in this place. She had decorated her walls with framed art of bright flowers on a white background, and there was a white bedside lamp. The walls were the same dark, warm wood as my room, but the contrasting colors made the space feel bigger and more cohesive.

Willow rolled to the other side of the room and my eyes nearly bugged out of my head when I saw her get up and walk to the desk. She must have seen my expression because she let out a small chuckle.

"Most people think everyone who uses a wheelchair is paralyzed, but that's not always the case." She grabbed a small notebook off the desk and walked back to me. "I'm an ambulatory wheelchair user, meaning I can walk short distances, but anything longer than a few yards, and I need the chair."

She took the washcloth from my fingers and replaced it with the notebook as she sat down beside me. I flipped it open and there were pages and pages filled with dates, times, and notes. I flipped to a random page and almost dropped the notebook. On the paper was a scribble of the symbol that was carved into

Bethany's hand, along with notes Willow had written regarding the symbol's origin.

"Something weird has been going on for a while," Willow explained. "It started a couple years ago, when I was a freshman. Several students died. All of them in my class, and each one had that symbol carved into their skin. I've been researching it nonstop, but I can't find anything about it. The most I've been able to gather is that it's called a sigil, as is the carving in the basement that opens the passage to the cavern. No one I've talked to in the Order knows what it is either, but my gut is telling me someone knows and isn't saying."

My finger ran back and forth over the drawing as Willow was talking, as if rubbing the sigil would somehow give me some answers.

I looked at Willow, and her eyes seemed to be somewhere else entirely. "You think whoever knows about the sigil is the one committing the murders?"

She closed her eyes, took a deep breath, and nodded.

I climbed further onto the bed, crossing my legs out in front of me, and flipped through a few more pages of the notebook. A name caught my eye, and I stopped to read the page.

I glanced back at Willow. "You know Dorian is Dhazor's son."

It wasn't a question, but once again, Willow nodded.

"I figured it out last year. I used to follow him around campus at night, and I witnessed him use his powers once. Against Dhazor, actually."

"Why don't you ask him what the sigil means?" I asked.

Wilow sighed. "He doesn't know that I know. Everyone in the Order knows something is weird with him, and I've asked other members about it. There's a theory going around that Dorian is Dhazor's spy, watching us so we don't do anything wild, but I don't think they know about his relation to Dhazor."

She seemed to think back on that last statement as she scooted onto the bed and crossed her legs. "Well, *most* of them might not know, but I think Odion and Joel do."

"Joel's a part of the Order?" I asked.

Willow nodded. I hadn't seen him in the cavern, but then again, most people still had hoods covering their faces when they left. I closed the notebook and sat up, hugging my knees to my chest, and debated telling Willow what I knew. She seemed so genuine in wanting to root out the murderer. I pursed my lips and decided I had to trust someone to help me. Before I could utter another word, though, I yawned, and my eyes didn't want to stay open. I checked the clock on her bedside table and groaned. Four in the morning. Thank God tomorrow — er, today — was Saturday.

I got off the bed and stretched. Willow yawned as well, and we decided to save the rest of the conversation for later. I trudged back to my room with my head reeling from the night's events. It didn't stop my body from sleeping though, because as soon as my head hit the pillow, I fell into unconsciousness.

I awoke at noon feeling rested, but weary. This was not how I expected my sophomore year of high school to go, and all I wanted to do was check on Dorian and Odion. I got changed, forgetting that I had fallen asleep in the black pants that were covered in Odion's blood, and headed out the door.

Alisa wasn't in the common room, but there was a small box on the coffee table addressed to me. I quickly opened it and sagged with relief. It was the phone Mom promised she'd send me. She must have overnighted it. I sent her a quick text thanking her and went to the other side of the building to check on the boys.

Joel answered the door when I knocked. He sported a scowl and a black eye. Fresh from the looks of it.

"Go away," he sneered. "Haven't you caused us enough trouble?"

I blinked once. Twice. "I just wanted to check on them."

Joel scoffed. "Dorian and Odion? What makes you think they'd want you around?"

His hostility made me take a physical step back. "I'm sorry."

"You should be. If you hadn't interfered last night, neither of them would have gotten hurt, but you just had to be where no one wants you. Like last summer. You weren't even supposed to go home that day, were you? You were supposed to go straight to that summer camp of yours."

My heart stopped. "How — how do you know that?"

Joel clamped his mouth shut, like he too realized he shouldn't have that information.

He started to slam the door in my face, but a hand jutted out from behind Joel and stopped it.

Joel had the decency to look embarrassed as Dorian came into view, opened the door wide, and motioned for me to come inside. I slid past Joel and, without a word, Dorian made a beeline for his room. I followed, and once we were alone, uncertainty descended like a cloud. My fingers fidgeted as I glanced around the room. Nothing had changed since the last time I had been in here, and yet, everything felt different.

Dorian sat on the edge of the bed and regarded me with a mixture of wariness and something I couldn't quite place. It almost looked like anger.

I strolled over to the small bookcase next to the desk. I picked up a random book and almost giggled.

"What's funny?" Dorian's voice sounded closer than it should have been.

I turned, and my breath caught. He was standing inches from me. I hadn't even heard him move, but his scent of fresh earth and wood filled my nostrils, and any response I was going to give went out the window. He inched closer, brushing the book that I still grasped. I swerved around him, and his features turned amused as he turned and tracked my movement.

"You haven't answered my question, Bubbles," he said. "What's so funny?"

I held up the book. "*Dante's Inferno*?"

Dorian chuckled darkly and took a calculated step toward me. "I find that book to be the most... accurate portrayal of demons."

"I don't," I said.

Dorian took another step as he raised an eyebrow. "And how many demons have you come across exactly?"

I pretended to think about the answer, but we both knew what it was. "Two, although one is an enormous dick and one confuses the hell out of me."

Dorian pursed his lips, and I could tell it was from trying not to laugh. He took two more steps, and I took a step backward. His eyes darkened.

"And which one am I?" He took yet another step in my direction.

I took two steps back and bumped into the dresser. I had no more room to move. Dorian smiled and leisurely closed in. While I was mad at him for not telling me crucial details, or any details really, I also wanted to be near him. I knew he was mad at me too, but I shoved that thought aside as I made a move to skirt around him. His arms snaked out, wrapping around me and securing my body against his. His lips were at my ear, and his breath tickled.

"Which demon am I?" he asked again.

I quirked up one half of my lip. "Right now? It could go either way."

Dorian nibbled my earlobe, and I clamped my mouth shut. I wasn't going to let him know I was enjoying this little game. He smiled despite my effort to hide my emotions, and his lips moved to the edge of my jaw. My eyes fluttered closed.

"I'm mad at you," I muttered.

"And I'm mad at you." Dorian gently kissed my neck right at the spot where my pulse was. "My, my, your heart is beating fast. Are you nervous being around me, or is this a reaction from desire?"

It was a struggle to get my head on straight, but I knew we had to iron this out, so I wriggled out of his grasp and looked him in the eye.

"Dorian, this is serious. We need to talk about what happened."

His face hardened. "Fine. Let's hear it."

I inhaled. "Why didn't you tell me you were part of the Divine Order?"

"Because you were never supposed to know about the Order at all. How did you find the cavern? And don't feed me that same lie from last night."

"Someone in the Order told me."

Dorian squeezed his eyes shut as he paced the room and muttered a string of curse words.

I placed my hands on my hips. "Why is that such a big deal?"

Dorian raised an eyebrow. "Other than it allowed you to put yourself in danger last night?"

I threw my hands up. "I did that because you wouldn't tell me anything!"

"I tried to!" Dorian screamed. "At the library! You didn't want to hear it, so why should I bother trying again?"

"Because that's what couples do, Dorian. They talk." My voice broke, and Dorian sighed.

He wrapped his arms around me and kissed the top of my head.

"Are we a couple?"

I looked up at him through my lashes. "I mean, I want to be... if you want it."

I had never seen Dorian's eyes so full of warmth. Instead of answering me with words, he stooped down and brushed his lips against mine. The tiniest of touches, but it was all the answer I needed.

When Dorian looked at me again, his face was full of pain.

"I want that," he said. "I still don't know how it's going to work when my dad thinks you're his, but we'll figure that out later. Right now though, it sounds like Odion is awake."

Chapter Fourteen

D ORIAN, JOEL, AND I were lounging in Odion's room while Odion sat propped up in bed. He looked like hell, with a gauze pad taped to the side of his head and bruises all over his face and torso. Odion's room was like every other room on campus, but the color scheme was vastly different. He had painted over the paneling with a dark gray color, and the walls and ceiling were pitch black. He chose a much lighter gray for the carpet, bringing a sense of openness to the space. The bed was huge and covered in more neutral tones. The desk sat right next to the bed frame and on the other side of the bed was a small nightstand that housed an even smaller lamp that dimly illuminated the surrounding area.

We were discussing about the previous night when Joel's phone dinged. He took one look at the screen and sighed.

"I have to go. It's urgent." He turned and left the room without another word.

Odion and Dorian exchanged exasperated glances. I looked between them, a frown forming on my face.

"What is it?" I asked.

They exchanged another glance, and an entire conversation seemed to take place with just a few expressions.

Dorian finally sighed and turned to me. "Don't trust Joel. If he asks you anything, just say you don't know."

"But why?"

Dorian ran his hands through his hair. "It's complicated."

Odion snorted as he adjusted his position in bed. "He's your father's spy. What's complicated about that?"

My jaw dropped slightly, and Dorian rolled his head back like they had had this conversation a million times before. Willow had been wrong. Others in the Order knew about Dorian's parentage.

"Half of the people in the Order are my father's spies," Dorian said. "Why is Joel being one of them a surprise?"

I stood from the desk chair I had sat in and put my hands in a T position.

"Okay, timeout. I thought *all* the Order members worshipped Dhazor?"

Odion laughed and clutched his side while Dorian tried to hide his smile.

"I don't," Odion said.

Dorian stood from the edge of the bed and wrapped his arms around me.

"My dad would love to think that everyone in the world worshipped him," Dorian said. "The truth is, though, a lot of the current members are what they call 'currency members.'"

I angled my head toward him. "Currency members?"

Odion groaned as he adjusted his posture again. "Meaning our parents passed the membership down to us as payment to Dhazor."

My nose crinkled. "That's disgusting."

"I agree," Dorian said.

Odion's face contorted in pain, and I grabbed the bottle of pain reliever off the nightstand and handed him two tablets, along with the glass of water next to the bottle. Odion popped the tablets into his mouth with a grateful smile and gulped down the entire contents of the glass. Setting the empty glass back on the table, I sat on the bed and turned so I faced both him and Dorian.

"How does someone actually become a member if they aren't, you know, born into it?"

Dorian caught my meaning immediately, and a sound came from his throat that I'm pretty sure was demonic.

"Absolutely not." His voice was like a blade forged of ice. "Last night was a one-off. You will never be down in the catacombs again."

"Catacombs?" I asked. "I thought it was just a cavern."

Odion smirked. "Oops. Looks like lover boy let something slip."

Dorian whipped his unyielding gaze to Odion and thrust his finger at me.

"She will not be a part of this."

Odion shrugged. "She already is. Besides, like last night, she'll do it on her own. It's for the best if she has people like us to watch her back when she does."

I crossed my legs and snapped my fingers twice. "Are you two men done making my decisions for me, or do we still need to discuss my dowry?"

They both had the decency to look at least slightly embarrassed. Dorian shook his head and sauntered over to the bed. He leaned down, pressing his hands into the mattress to look at both me and Odion at eye level.

"I. Said. No."

My jaw clenched. "Odion's right. I'm already a part of this, and I can help stop Dhazor." I leaned back on the mattress, resting my weight on my locked arms. "Unless you want me to just sit back and let him make me your new mommy."

Dorian's face went green, and I actually thought he might throw up on the bed. I was right there with him, but I wouldn't let my disgust at the thought deter me. He went over to the large window and stared out at the New England scenery. It was raining today, and the gloomy sky only added to the room's cool atmosphere.

"She can help, Dor." Odion's gentle voice must have been convincing, because a moment later Dorian sighed and marched toward me.

He put my hands over his chest and squeezed them tightly. His heart thrummed erratically, and his molten eyes bore into mine with such intensity, I thought they would suck me into them.

"You need to put on a show," Dorian said. "Let Dhazor think you're open to the idea of... being his."

He said that last part with difficulty, like it physically pained him to get the words out, and I knew the feeling.

"And," he continued, "do not let him or the Order suspect anything. Dhazor may have claimed you, but if he thinks you'll betray him, he won't hesitate to kill you."

A nod was my only answer. I meant what I had told Dorian in his room the night after Bethany died. I would be the first to say no to Dhazor and live. In fact, I would be the first to make Dhazor beg for death.

A plan formulated in my head overnight. Find a member of the Order and convince them to let me join. It sounded simple enough, but I had to be careful which member I asked. Dorian said that half the members were spies for Dhazor, but I had no idea which members were in the Order because they wanted to be, versus which ones were only there as Dhazor's payment.

I replayed the night in the cavern — er, catacombs — and figured that even though Alisa was the easiest one to track down, she was probably not the best one to ask. I could have asked Harper, the redhead who stood up to Alisa, but then again, she almost turned me into a human sacrifice. Rachel was also a no go. She was more of a bitch than Alisa, and even if she wasn't a spy for Dhazor, I doubt she would help me anyway. Odion and Joel would listen to Dorian, so I couldn't ask them either. The tall brunette guy with highlights intimidated me. Besides, I didn't know his name or where to find him. Same with the rest of the members. They hadn't taken off their hoods, so their identities were a mystery.

By the time I knew who I wanted to ask, it was the middle of the afternoon, but I knocked on Willow's door anyway, hoping she would be in her dorm. One of her roommates answered. She was short with strawberry blond hair and her deep brown eyes regarded me warily before calling for Willow. She ushered me inside just as Willow was stepping out of her room. The strawberry blond girl plopped on the couch and started scrolling on her phone.

"Ophelia!" Willow smiled warmly and tossed her straight black hair over her shoulder as she wrapped her arms around me. When we broke the embrace, her smile turned downward. "Is everything okay?"

"I need a favor," I said.

Willow led me back to her room and sat on the bed cross-legged. I pulled out the chair from underneath the desk and scooted it in front of her.

"What's the favor?" she asked.

"I want to become an official member of the Divine Order."

Willow pulled her hair over her shoulder and scrunched her face. "You want to what?"

"You heard me."

"Did I? Because all I heard you saying was gibberish."

I put my hands in my lap and leaned forward. "I need to find out who killed Bethany. Besides, according to Dorian, Dhazor has already 'claimed' me, so I need to figure a way out of that, too, because that's disgusting and there's no way that's happening, and the only way I can figure out both things is if I am fully submerged into this demonic shit. Please, I need your help."

Willow pinched the bridge of her nose. "You want in the Order while I want *out* of it. How ironic."

I grabbed Willow's free hand, and she looked at me with her pale blue eyes.

"Help me get into the Order. Help me kill Dhazor, and you won't ever have to be in service to a demon ever again."

She shook her head, but it wasn't in disagreement. "You're being foolish, but okay. I'll call a meeting, and I'll let you know."

I squeezed her hand in thanks and left. Step one was underway. I had no idea what step two was or any step after that, but I would cross those bridges later.

My heart stopped as I walked into my English class the next day. Dhazor, or I guess in this setting he was Headmaster Keswick, sat behind the teacher's desk, and I mentally cursed myself for not remembering he was subbing all this week.

I silently took my seat and tried not to look at him, even when I could feel his eyes boring into me. The bell rang, signaling the start of class, and I took out my textbook, flipped to a random page about Mesopotamian literature and read the text without comprehending it.

Dhazor started the lecture. What it was actually about, I couldn't say, and I didn't care. The only thing I was paying attention to was the way my anger rose and rested just below the surface. Bethany died, the creep claimed me, and he slowly took people's lives so he could be young forever? I wanted to smack him, Divine Demon or not. Add in the fact that he hated his son so much because he was half human, and it took every ounce of self-control I had not to launch the six-pound textbook at his head.

Of course, if I did that, it would clue Dhazor in on the one thing I promised Dorian he would never suspect. And I would also probably die.

That would suck.

So I kept reminding myself that it was one hour of the day for one week, and I could handle it. The bell rang, and I gathered up my things and left so fast that I didn't notice I had forgotten my entire backpack until I was halfway to my next class.

Cursing myself, I turned back and halted when I saw the classroom was empty. And that Dhazor was going through my things.

"What are you doing?" My voice came out sharp, and I reminded myself to act like I liked the guy.

Dhazor leisurely zipped my backpack and turned to face me with a smile, as if he hadn't just been caught snooping through a student's belongings.

"I was just getting to know you better," he said.

"By searching through my stuff?"

Dhazor shrugged. "You won't talk to me. You didn't even look at me the entire class. That hurt, by the way. How else am I supposed to find things out about my future bride?"

Hearing the words from his mouth brought bile rising up my esophagus. I swallowed it back down, hoping he'd excuse it as me being nervous. In fact, I could use that. Swallowing again, I bit my bottom lip and slowly treaded closer to him.

"Future bride?" I asked.

Dhazor raised an eyebrow. "Don't act coy, it's unbecoming. I know my son has told you... things."

I took a step closer, trying to mimic the stance Dorian had with me the other night. It was more difficult than he made it look.

"Things like... you claiming me?"

Dhazor snorted and rolled his eyes. "He makes it sound like you have no say in the matter."

I took another step. "Do I?"

I was only a few feet from him now, and I looked up at him between my lashes as he stared down at me. From here, I could see his skin was getting sallow again and his hair was thinning. He needed another sacrifice soon, and I hoped he wouldn't get it.

"Of course, my dearest." His voice was gentle, like a lullaby.

His hand reached out, and he gently dragged his fingertips down the side of my cheek. Without my consent, my body leaned into the touch. The bell for the start of my next class rang, and I jolted away from him. I reached past Dhazor, yanked my backpack off the desk, and hurried to my next class without another word.

Chapter Fifteen

I TRIED NOT TO think about what happened between me and Dhazor at all over the course of the next few days, but my stomach felt queasy no matter how I distracted myself. After classes, I spent my time in Dorian's dorm doing as much homework as I physically could. Odion was slowly getting better, although the nurse hadn't cleared him yet. Dorian told me they used the excuse that Odion had gotten into a fight to explain his injuries. He could even get out of bed and lounge on the couch, which is where I found him one afternoon.

I plopped my backpack down on the floor and sighed as I threw myself into the leather armchair. Dorian and Joel were playing a round of billiards, and from the frustrated grunts Joel was making, I'd say Dorian was winning. While Joel was lining up his next shot, Dorian sprinted over and quickly dropped a kiss to the top of my head. I smiled and felt my body instantly relax.

They finished their game as I finished my geometry homework. As I predicted, Dorian had indeed won the game, and Joel slouched on the couch, pouting. I had finished the homework for all my subjects except English. Dorian perched himself on the arm of the chair as I wordlessly scowled at the required reading. He smoothed my hair back as I stared at the words, not comprehending a single syllable.

"Why don't we study in my room?" he suggested.

I looked into his eyes, and I saw a flash of concern before his expression smoothed into a smile. I gathered up my things, and he took them from me as the solace of the deep purple walls surrounded and calmed me.

Dorian set my backpack on his desk while I flopped down on the bed, staring at the ceiling. He lay next to me, and while he didn't touch me, it felt intimate just being this close to him. Turning my body toward his, I smiled. He didn't smile back.

"What's wrong?" I asked.

"I was about to ask you that same question."

My eyebrows knit together. "What do you mean?"

Dorian sighed. "Don't think I haven't noticed the shift in your mood the last few days. You were fine this past weekend. Pissed and determined as hell, but fine. And over the past few days, you've become increasingly distraught. Did Dhazor do something?"

I bit my lip and sat up. Dorian mimicked the movement and swept some hair behind my ear. I glanced at him, and his worried expression made a lump form in my throat. I told him about the conversation Dhazor and I had in the classroom, and Dorian growled. The sound wasn't human, and a chill seeped into my bones.

"Can — can he really make me be his?" My voice sounded so small.

"Technically, no. You have to accept his offer, but he can torture and kill everyone you love until you say yes."

"Why hasn't he asked me yet?"

Dorian looked toward the window and ran his hands through his hair. "I honestly don't know. Maybe he's waiting until you're no longer a suspect in Bethany's death, or maybe he's hoping you won't find out about that crucial detail."

My hands wound their way into the cream fabric of the bedspread. "Why would me being cleared matter?"

"It doesn't, but it's easier to accomplish things when the eyes of the police aren't on you."

I shuddered, and Dorian scooted over to me and cradled me against his chest.

"Whatever happens," he said, "I won't let him take you."

I smiled and inhaled his scent deeply. I drew away a couple of inches and memorized the features of his face. He seemed to do the same thing. I pulled his face to mine and kissed him passionately. Dorian slid his hands down to my waist and squeezed me to him so hard I momentarily couldn't breathe. His lips seized every part of my being, and fire raced through my veins.

When we broke apart, both of us were breathing hard. Dorian kissed my forehead, his lips lingering for several seconds until my phone buzzed in my pocket, effectively ending the moment.

I looked at the screen, and my heart thudded. "That was Willow. The Order is meeting in two days after school."

Dorian's face turned grim. "I'll try to convince them to let you in, but Ophelia, I hope you know what you're doing. Once you're a part of the Order, it's damn near impossible to get out."

I kissed his cheek and reassured him, but I hoped I knew what I was doing too.

Waiting was almost impossible. The meeting was over, but the Order either hadn't decided or Dorian hadn't told me what it was.

"Just be patient," he said one day after classes.

Easy for him to say. It had been three days since the meeting, and I was about ready to explode from the endless waiting.

Two days after that, I had just plopped my backpack on my bed after class when I heard someone close my bedroom door. I whipped my body around to find a small, yellowed envelope sealed with blood red wax on my dresser. The symbol pressed into the seal was similar to the sigil that was carved into Bethany's hand. My hands shook as I broke the seal and pulled out an aged piece of paper with one word written on it.

Soon

This had to be from the Order. They had finally decided and accepted me. My smile grew as I gently placed the paper back into the envelope and slid it underneath my mattress for safe-keeping. I couldn't focus on homework that night, and instead I paced the perimeter of the room until I was pretty sure I had marked a permanent path into the carpet.

My body finally got tired enough to sleep a little after one a.m. and as soon as my head hit the pillow, my door burst open.

I screamed as three people in maroon hoods rushed in and grabbed me. One person held me down on the mattress as the other two gagged me and bound my hands together. The person who had held me then threw a burlap bag over my head, and the three of them guided me to what I assumed were the catacombs. I heard the secret passage grind open, and after another minute or two, they pushed me onto my knees and removed the burlap.

Candles littered every open space, casting the walls in a dancing orange pattern, and I blinked up at eleven people, all in hoods. The Divine Order.

Dorian lowered his hood as he knelt and undid my bonds.

"Sorry for the theatrics," he said. "Secret society and all."

He winked at me as he helped me to my feet and, one by one, the members of the order removed their hoods. I recognized a lot of them. Alisa, Rachel, Joel, Odion, and Willow I already knew were a part of the Order. Then there was Harper, the redhead who had stood up to Alisa on Halloween. Had that really only been two weeks ago?

No one else spoke. They all just stared at me with varying degrees of annoyance. I gave an awkward wave as Alisa came forward, her expression almost disdainful.

"If it were up to me, you wouldn't even know about any of this, much less be a part of it. However, the Order has taken a vote and you're in. *If* you can complete three simple tasks by sunrise."

I had a feeling these tasks were going to be anything but simple, but I was mistaken.

Willow rolled forward, almost running Alisa's foot over, and earning herself a murderous glare.

"Your first task will be to find this." She handed me a folded piece of white printer paper.

I unfolded it and knit my eyebrows. "So I just need to locate a... half-eaten chicken wing?"

Alisa snatched the paper from my hand. "It's obviously a key."

The group stifled their laughs, and Alisa rolled her eyes.

"You need to find a skeleton key," Willow said, "and the only hint we can give you is it's somewhere on campus."

I snatched the paper back from Alisa with a smirk. Find a key. That was easy enough.

It was not easy.

I spent two hours searching the building and came up empty-handed. They wouldn't have put it in someone's dorm, would they? I plopped down on the steps leading to the exit of the main building and looked through the window above the double doors of the academy. A sliver of the moon was just peeking through drifting clouds. If I didn't get this first task done soon, there was no way I'd be able to complete the other two in time.

I thought back to everything I had learned about Dhazor and the society so far. Where would they keep an old, demonic skeleton key? I swore under my breath as I figured out exactly where to look.

I snuck into the main office as quietly as I could and swore again when the door to Dhazor's office was locked.

"What are you doing?"

I pivoted to find Dorian leaning against the wall opposite me.

"I'm looking for the damn key. What do you think?"

Dorian raised an eyebrow at my sharp tone. He pushed off the wall and grabbed me around the waist, pulling me close to his chest.

"It's not in there," he whispered.

I sighed. "Then where is it?"

Dorian's soft laugh reverberated through me. "Don't spoil the mood, Bubbles. And don't stress either. You'll often find that a house made of glass breaks."

I was about to tell him off for calling me weak, but he had a gleam in his eyes that made me pause. He wasn't telling me I was weak. He was giving me a hint! But what did houses of glass and me spoiling the mood have to do with anything? Dorian kept me close to him and brushed some hair out of my face while I was deep in thought.

I gasped as I finally figured it out and wriggled out of Dorian's grasp. Dashing out of the office toward the entrance of the school, I halted and backtracked when I realized I hadn't thanked Dorian. He was facing the door with his arms crossed when I burst back in and kissed him with as much passion as I could muster. His arm snaked around my waist and pulled me closer for a moment before letting go.

"Thank you," I murmured against his lips.

"You're welcome. Now go."

My feet raced out the main doors and toward the back of campus. The dilapidated greenhouse came into view, and I rested my hands on my knees to catch my breath for a minute before forcing my legs to move again.

The wooden door hung on one crooked hinge and looked like someone had once painted it a brilliant blue, but the paint was now faded and chipped. The brass handle popped off in my hand as I tried to pull the door open, but there was a hole large enough where I figured I could squeeze through.

It was a tight fit, but once I was inside, I frantically searched for the key by toppling over old terra-cotta pots and pulling overgrown ivy that had made its way in through the broken glass walls. I pushed a large pot full of dirt in the corner over onto its side and heard a dull thud.

I ran my hands through the old soil and felt something long and rough. The key! Brushing the dirt off, the first thing I noticed was how cold it felt in my hand. The second thing almost made me drop the key back onto the ground. It wasn't metal. The skeleton key was made of bone.

Aged and yellowed, the surface was rough in my palm. A row of beautifully carved roses made up the bow of the key, and the only thing marring the design was the skull in the middle. Two small rubies glistened in the eye sockets, and they seemed to stare into my very soul. As I stuffed the needed object into my pocket, I hoped whoever had carved the key hadn't used human bone.

Back in the catacombs, Alisa was lounging on a ledge, her leg swinging. The rest of the members were standing or sitting in clusters. I presented Alisa with the key and her face turned into a sneer, but Dorian and Willow glowed with pride.

"What's the second task?" I asked.

Harper now came up to me. "Your second and third tasks are simple. Find what the key fits and bring us back the object emblazoned with Dhazor's sigil."

I groaned.

"Or you could give up now." Rachel's voice carried from a small group of members standing around in the back of the cavern.

I gave her the sweetest smile I could muster and flipped my hair behind my shoulder.

"Why give up? I know exactly where this key goes."

I silently cursed myself as I made my way up the stairs that led out of the basement because I didn't actually know where the key went. I just wanted to get under Rachel's skin, and from the shade of red she turned, I had accomplished my mission.

I sat outside under the soft glow of a lamppost and studied the key. Other than the creep factor of it being made from actual bone, it didn't look any different from any other skeleton keys I'd seen.

My dad had a collection of skeleton keys in his office, and while each one was designed a little differently, they were built the same.

"They may seem the same, but each key is unique to its lock. Just like you," he said.

"But I thought the whole point of a skeleton key was it could open anything."

Dad knelt so we were at eye level. "Nothing has access to everything. The trick with a skeleton key is to know which locks it can access, and which ones it can't."

"How will I be able to tell the difference?" I asked.

Dad chuckled and pressed a kiss to my forehead. "Look for patterns in the design. They might be subtle, but they're there."

The soft timbre of Dad's voice echoed through my head, and I couldn't stop the images that ran through my mind. The way his muscular arms used to toss me in the air as a kid, or the way his hair was the same shade of sandy blond as mine, or...

The muscles in my face clenched and relaxed a few seconds later. Each part of my body tightened one area at a time as I grounded myself back into the present. I wouldn't let myself think about what had happened. I had a task to focus on.

Staring at the key again, I tried to notice a pattern, and something about the key felt oddly familiar, like I had seen the matching lock before. I closed my eyes and thought back to every interaction I've had with the Order, but nothing rang a bell. I had a vague memory of Dorian using a similar key... I hurled myself off the cold bench and sprinted out of the academy's front gate, not stopping to wonder why it was open in the middle of the night.

I reached the public library in record time. The lights in the small building were on, and someone had left the front door cracked. I entered and jogged all the way to the large ornate door in the back. The roses that adorned the thick wood were the same design as the bow of the key.

I didn't hesitate as I slid the key into the lock and turned. The chunky click of the deadbolt reverberated through the empty building, and I made my way down into the basement of books. I strolled over to the shelf that housed the book Dorian and I had looked at the last time we were down here.

The same jolt went through me when I picked it up. This had to be Dhazor's sigil. It had pictures of him and names of past aliases. Almost like a journal. I was about to head back to the catacombs when I remembered something else that was in this book. Setting it on the table, I quickly thumbed through the pages until I found what I was looking for, and ripped the page out, hastily stuffing it into my pocket.

The sky was lightening with the threat of dawn as I raced back into the school and down the stairs that led to the passageway. Five of the members, including Rachel, were asleep as I slid to a stop in the middle of the cavern and slammed the book down on the ground with a loud thud. Rachel jerked awake, and her look of pure hatred was reward enough, but Alisa bent down to pick up the ancient book and glanced at me with little emotion.

"Welcome to the Divine Order, Ophelia Allan."

WINTER

Chapter Sixteen

THE DAY BEFORE WINTER break was hectic, to say the least. Teachers trying to cram in last-minute lectures, students packing to go home for two weeks, and the Divine Order needing to complete a sacrifice by midnight.

Infiltration of the Order was slow going. Even though most of the members didn't want to be there, they still had a hard time trusting me and opening up. It didn't help that only a select few could even know why I was in the Order to begin with. The rest thought I was Dhazor's golden girl and Dorian's plaything.

The labels bothered me very little. I had two missions while I was in the Order. Find Beth's killer and destroy Dhazor. Everything else seemed trivial. Finding him a sacrifice wasn't part of the plan, but Dorian convinced me to go along with it since we didn't have the information or evidence needed for either of my goals.

The student the Order picked out was an introverted boy who was planning to go home for the holidays that evening instead of shuttling with the rest of the students in the morning. We had the meeting about it two nights prior and had decided that, as the newest member, it would be my responsibility to lure the boy into the catacombs.

I hated the idea. Every fiber of my being screamed in protest, and I wanted to throw up just thinking about it. I reminded myself several times that even though he was called a sacrifice, he wouldn't die. His life would just be shortened. By how much I didn't know, and I wasn't sure I wanted to.

But I did what I was supposed to do. I walked up to him after the last bell rang, batted my eyelashes, and led him down to the basement. Odion, Joel, and the member with brown and blond highlighted hair, whose name I'd learned was Elijah, tied the boy up and kept him from struggling as we descended the stairs to the catacombs. The sacrificial room was off to the left of the cavern through another secret door, and the rest of the Order already had everything set up. I donned my maroon cloak and pulled the hood over my head.

The ritual itself was a bit involved as each member had to stand around the sacrifice, who was now on his knees in the middle of a circle drawn in chalk, cut their palm open, and spill exactly three drops of blood each into a golden goblet.

Willow led the ritual, and after we all had done our part, I watched in fascination as she walked into the middle of the circle and knelt before the boy. Tears were streaming down his face, and Joel had gagged him when he wouldn't stop begging for us to stop. Willow lifted the dagger we all took turns using and sliced a fast, clean cut across the boy's forearm.

Blood quickly seeped through the split in his skin, and Willow slid the goblet under the gash, and tipped his arm so the thick crimson liquid flowed effortlessly. The blood hit the halfway mark quickly, and Willow raised the goblet in the air, the gold shimmering under the firelight.

Shadows engulfed the room. At first, it seemed like the fire was still flickering, causing the shadows to dance, but then a figure took shape. A moment later, Dhazor was fully corporeal. He wore a dark black suit with a deep maroon cloak fastened in the front with his sigil, and just like that first night I met him, his skin was gray and sunken, and his hair was lifeless.

He seemed to glide into the middle of the circle, stopping right next to the boy, and took the goblet from Willow's outstretched hands. Dhazor drank the contents, making my stomach churn, and the circle drawn in front of us glowed an eerie red.

The boy screamed through his gag. Dhazor's face filled out, and his hair thickened. When the glowing light of the circle faded, Dhazor looked like the picture of perfect health, and the boy was unconscious.

Dhazor kicked the boy's body out of the circle, and I flinched as he addressed us.

"My loyal followers, thank you for once again helping me." He turned to me. "And lovely Ophelia, I'm so glad you've joined the Order. I can only hope this means you'll consider my other proposition as well."

I steeled my expression into neutral, and he winked as he melted into shadows and left.

The wails of an innocent echoed through my mind that night, and I was groggy as I walked into the cafeteria the next morning. Dorian greeted me with a cup of orange juice and a quick kiss. I smiled up at him as I took the juice and gulped it down, the sweet tang waking up my brain.

I've never been a huge coffee drinker. The most caffeine I'd ever consumed was an extra-large soda at the movie theater, but that morning I was contemplating drinking the entire pot brewing on the back table.

The excited chatter of students waiting for the academy shuttle to take them to the airport was making my head pound as I piled fresh scrambled eggs and a waffle on my plate. Several members of the Order were staying behind, including me, Willow, Alisa, and Joel. Dorian was, of course, staying because he had nowhere else to go, but the rest of the members were heading home for the holidays. A pang of jealousy ran through me at the thought as Dorian led me to an empty table in the back of the room. We sat next to each other, so close our knees brushed.

I had barely taken a bite of my waffle when the PA system crackled to life and Ms. Crane announced the shuttles were ready for boarding. Loud cheers erupted, and the students stampeded out of the room, leaving me, Dorian, and a few other students behind. One by one, the students filed out until Dorian and I were the only ones left. The silence was welcome, and Dorian seemed to notice my change in demeanor. He slung an arm around me and pulled me close. I snuggled into him, basking in his presence that was both calming and exhilarating.

I yelped as he tickled me with his free hand, and I tried to wriggle away, only for him to tighten his grasp and tickle my sides more. He was trying to cheer me up, and if he wanted to play that game...

My hands lifted the hem of his shirt as I tried to tickle him back, but other than a slight giggle, I didn't break him.

"This is where we eat, you know."

Dorian and I pulled away from each other and smoothed our clothes as Willow rolled over to our table with her own plate of food.

I was still smiling, and I could tell by the gleam in Dorian's eyes that he was still in a lighthearted mood as well. My headache was gone, even though my eyes still felt heavy.

"There's no one else in here." I popped another bite of my waffle into my mouth.

She snorted as she ate a spoonful of cereal. "*I'm* in here. If you two wanna do that, take it outside." She seemed to think about her last statement. "Or better yet, keep it inside. In a room. With no one else in it."

Dorian stared directly at Willow and tucked me under his arm a little more, and she gave him a solitary finger in return.

My mind turned toward Dhazor, and Dorian lifted my chin and gave me a questioning look. I waved it off, but I knew he wasn't going to give up.

"That boy last night, is he really okay?" I asked.

I directed the question at Dorian, but Willow shifted in her chair and answered. "He's... he'll be fine."

I wiggled out of Dorian's embrace and looked between the two of them. "What do you mean 'he'll be fine'? I thought the sacrifice didn't die right away."

"They don't," Dorian said, "but that doesn't mean the ritual isn't hard on them physically as well as mentally. You saw how he reacted last night. Even if the sacrifices don't remember details, they know something happened to them."

"That's cruel." I looked down at my food with no appetite anymore.

"That's the way it is." Willow had a bitter edge to her voice, and I didn't blame her.

A voice echoed from behind us. I turned in my chair and watched Alisa as she bounced up to our table and sat down next to Willow. Since we were the only ones in the room, I knew she had overheard the conversation.

"And you're okay with that." I didn't phrase it like a question, but Alisa answered anyway.

"Of course. And if you're not, you shouldn't be in the Order."

A thinly veiled threat. Alisa was one member who truly didn't mind being a part of the Order. If she or anyone in the Order thought I wasn't all in, I'd probably be the next sacrifice. And like Bethany, I wouldn't last through one ritual. I wondered what else she would do to please Dhazor. Dorian nudged me with his knee. It was barely a touch, but he was telling me to be careful.

"I'm not saying I'm not okay with it," I said, "but wouldn't it be less suspicious if the school wasn't crawling with people who we sacrificed?"

Alisa raised an eyebrow. "That's why we only use one sacrifice at a time."

I laid my hands on the table, interlacing my fingers, and hunched my shoulders, trying to look worried and meek. "But Bethany —"

"Couldn't handle the physical or mental stress of the ritual." Alisa interrupted. "It was a complete accident."

Her tone was sharp, and Dorian nudged me again. Enough.

"I know. It's just I'm still a suspect in her m — death, and I'm worried."

Alisa narrowed her eyes for a second, probably contemplating whether or not to believe me. She finally rested her hand on top of mine and squeezed gently.

"You're one of us now. We'll protect you." Alisa leaned back and flipped her bleached hair over her shoulder. "Besides, you always have Dhazor's offer. I bet being his has its own set of perks."

Another challenge. She was trying to find any weak spot she could. Willow tried to get my attention, but I ignored her and Dorian as I focused solely on Alisa's gaze.

"I've been thinking about that, actually," I said.

Dorian blanched. I continued to ignore him.

"And?" Alisa asked.

"And, while I respect our Divine Demon Lord, I'm not sure I'm ready for that sort of commitment. Yet."

Alisa scoffed and stood, scooping up her tray of barely eaten food. "Eventually, Ophelia, you'll have to make a choice. It's *him*" — she pointed her chin in Dorian's direction — "or Dhazor. You can't have them both."

She pivoted away from us so fast I thought she was going to slip and fall, but she just made a beeline for the side exit, dropping her tray with the others on her way out.

Willow rolled her chair back and forth several times, and Dorian wouldn't meet my eyes.

"What is it?" I asked.

"She's right." Willow whispered.

"No, she's not." My jaw clenched and my fingers tightened.

Dorian still wouldn't look at me, but when I turned my whole body to face him, he sighed.

"She *is* right. You'll have to make a choice. You can accept Dhazor's... offer and we'll no longer be a couple, or you can go against him. Choose that option, however, and your life, and the lives of everyone you love, will be in danger until you die. Or until he's enamored with someone else and forgets you, but I honestly don't think that will happen."

I took Dorian's chin between my fingers and gently forced him to look at me. His eyes were full of pain, but they held something else, and that one expression knocked the air out of my lungs. I brought his lips to mine and tried to express my feelings through that kiss. When we broke apart, his eyes were wet, and if I hadn't already made my decision, my choice would've been clear in that moment.

"The plan is still the same," I whispered. "We kill Dhazor, and I stay with you. No one else dies."

Dorian's lips turned up into what I thought was trying to be a smile, but looked more like a grimace.

"We should go shopping tomorrow."

I jumped at Willow's voice. I had forgotten she was sitting only a few feet from us. It was strange. When Dorian and I were together, it felt as if the entire world melted away.

I turned back in my chair to face her. "Shopping? Why?"

She looked at me like I had grown two heads. "Why not? We have no classes, and I haven't been away from the academy in forever."

Dorian kissed my temple as he picked up all three of our trays. I stood up and stretched my legs.

"That sounds like fun," he said.

Willow gave him a too-sweet smile. "Sorry, girls only."

He snorted. "You're a girl? I didn't notice."

I laughed as Willow tried to run Dorian over with her wheelchair, and as we exited the cafeteria, making plans for the next day, I saw a pair of multicolored eyes in the corner melt into shadows.

Chapter Seventeen

A FRESH BLANKET OF snow covered the ground as I stood by the front gates of Raven's Cove Academy. Dark gray clouds covered the sky, making the white landscape feel ominous yet serene. The bitter breeze was biting through my admittedly not warm enough sweater. I had expected New England to be cold, but this was Antarctic-level freezing. I would have to pick up some warmer clothes when we were in town.

Willow met me outside a few moments later just as the school shuttle arrived. The school was within walking distance of the main town of Ashton, but since Willow couldn't walk that far, and using her wheelchair on slick ground was probably not the smartest idea, we opted to take a ride.

The shuttle dropped us off near Main Street, and once Willow was in her chair, she made a beeline for a small boutique. I followed as quickly as I could manage, but while Ashton was good about keeping the roads clear of snow, there were still slick spots on the sidewalk.

Warm air scented with vanilla and cinnamon wafted into my face as we entered the small shop. Clear crystal chandeliers hung in various places, and the light refracted into rainbows that danced along the yellowish-beige walls. Color-coded clothes hung on rows of racks. Willow went one way, and I went the opposite direction. We found several things to try on and even found a few articles of clothing for each other. A couple of hours later, we left the store with several bags and almost no money left.

The shuttle wouldn't pick us up for another couple of hours, so we agreed to stop for some lunch before heading back to the academy. The restaurant we chose was tiny, as were a lot of the places around Ashton, and the atmosphere was warm and cozy. Fake moss hung on the walls, and the paint that did peek through was a baby blue color. Pink leather booths lined the walls, and flameless candles sat in the middle of every table, giving the atmosphere an open and modern vibe.

We sat at a table so Willow could have easy access, and I spent the rest of the money I had allotted for today on a California roll and crab rangoon. Willow ordered a bunch of sashimi and an appetizer of raw calamari and vegetables. I crinkled my nose when the server brought it out. Willow laughed.

"You don't like sushi?" she asked as she popped a tentacle in her mouth.

I was pretty sure I turned a nasty shade of green. "Raw anything doesn't belong in the human body."

Willow giggled again. "What about steak?"

I pulled apart a rangoon and started eating it from the middle out. "Well done with a ton of ketchup."

Willow scrunched her face and shook her head. "You heathen."

We both laughed, but Willow's face turned contemplative.

"What's wrong?" I asked.

She ate a piece of sashimi. "I was just thinking about yesterday. If you really want to take Dhazor down, you'll need help."

I gulped down some water and sighed. "I know, but it seems like everyone around here adores him."

"Most of the Order doesn't," she reminded me.

"That's because they had no say in the matter."

"True."

"So," I asked, "who can help besides the people that Dhazor is watching?"

Willow finished her sushi. "There's an old man who runs a shop around here. His name is Ernest, and as much as Dhazor has tried, he can't get the old man to adore him."

"Why would Dhazor care about one person's opinion?"

"Ernest has... abilities that normal humans don't," Willow explained, "and those abilities would be pretty useful to someone like Dhazor."

Popping my last crab rangoon in my mouth, I remembered a few weeks ago when I visited the shop. I've never been able to forget the smell of decay on his breath, or the things he said to me that still haunted my dreams. I had been trying to piece those words together since that day, but nothing made sense to me. Especially the part about "her acolytes." *Whose* acolytes?

Willow seemed to know a lot about the guy, so maybe she knew what he was talking about.

"I've met him," I said. "He seems nice."

"He is. He was the first one around here to make me feel like I wasn't a burden because I can't walk."

I bit my lip. Maybe now wasn't the right time to bring up what Ernest told me. Willow had a haunted look in her eyes.

"Do you want to talk about it?"

She gave me a small smile. "You know, you're the first person to ask that. Mostly, everyone wants to avoid the topic, but someone attacked me when I was seven. My mom had just gone to the store and my dad was working in the office we had at home. I was watching *Sesame Street* when a strange man broke in the front door. I remember screaming, and a sharp pain going through my back. The attacker had a bat, and my dad came rushing out of the office."

Willow swallowed hard. "They struggled, and my dad got the bat, but the man who broke in pulled a gun and shot my dad point blank. I was lying on the floor, crying and screaming. The man pointed the gun at me, but luckily that's when the cops showed up. Apparently, he was a fugitive and there had been this huge manhunt. My neighbor had recognized him and called 911."

Willow wiped away a few tears, and I sniffled, the story hitting a little too close to home.

"The doctor told my mom I was lucky. That the man had hit me with the bat and broke a couple of vertebrae, but I wasn't completely paralyzed. It was still a long road, and a vertebra didn't heal quite right. Hence, the chair."

She made a sweeping motion over her and her wheelchair.

"What about your dad?" My voice cracked because I was pretty sure I knew the answer.

"Died instantly," she said. "That's when Mom pledged herself, and me, to Dhazor. She just... wanted to stop hurting."

I clenched my hands together under the table. "Did he stop her pain?"

Willow shook her head. "I mean, I guess having a 'higher power' to idolize comforted her, but no. There was no magic spell, no ritual. She still cries herself to sleep sometimes."

The server came over with our check, and thankfully we didn't have the relive any more horrible memories.

The cold seemed even more chilling as we left the restaurant. Willow and I didn't talk about much as we made our way to Ernest's shop. There was no sign saying the shop name, but Willow told me it was called Aura and Earth, which seemed fitting. I hadn't yet brought up my visit to the shop, or the creepy prophecy Ernest had given me, but since we were about to talk to the guy, I figured he could provide some clarification.

We were about to walk inside when Willow's phone rang. She stayed outside to answer it, and I made my way into the dimly lit store. The scent was the same as last time, incense that smelled like a church, only there was another smell too. It smelled sour and sweet and the deeper I moved into the shop, the stronger the smell got. It reminded me of my twelfth birthday when Dad took me and my mom camping. There had been a lake, and the scent that wafted from it was sweet, but somehow rotten, like a bunch of apples had gone bad.

I heard a faint hum coming from the back that wasn't present the last time I was in here, and I went to check it out.

"Ernest?" I called.

No answer.

The humming got louder as I neared the beaded curtain that led to the back. The smell hit me directly then. I gagged and my eyes watered. I covered my nose, and beads clacked as I moved them out of the way and froze.

Slouched in one of the two chairs was Ernest. His eyes were open and glassed over, staring at nothing. His mouth gaped. A bug flew into my face. I swatted it away, and that was when I realized the humming noise I heard wasn't humming at all. There were about a dozen flies buzzing around the room and crawling over his body.

Ernest was dead.

My feet trudged forward, but I felt a million miles away. The buzzing became a roaring. Blood pounded in my ears. Something was sticking out of his chest, but I didn't know what. I grabbed hold of it and pulled. Initially, whatever it was stuck a little, but with a sickening squelch, it slid free. I stared at the knife in my hand, the blade coated with thick blood.

I knocked another fly away, and Ernest's hand caught my eye. It was situated, palm up, on the arm of the chair, and the same symbol that was in Willow's journal, the same symbol that was carved into Bethany's hand, was also carved into Ernest's.

I backed away, bumping into the table so hard I knocked several things off. Picking them up as fast as I could, I arranged them back on the table, not wanting to disturb the crime scene, and made my way to the front of the store. I was reaching for the door to tell Willow when it burst open, almost hitting me in the nose. I jerked back and came face to face with Detective Zachary Russo. His wide eyes shifted from mine to the knife, and his expression instantly shifted.

"Put the knife down, Ophelia." His command was low, but firm.

I glanced down, and sure enough, I still held the knife I pulled out of Ernest's chest. I uncurled my fingers, and the knife clattered to the ground. Detective Russo grabbed me and shoved me around, pulling both of my arms behind my back.

"Ophelia Allan, you are under arrest for the murder of Bethany Woods."

Another officer emerged from the back room. I didn't even see him come inside, but something in his expression must have told Detective Russo everything he needed.

"And," he continued, "for the murder of Ernest Elrod."

Being back in the police station wasn't an ideal start to my winter vacation, and yet, the sterile atmosphere of the interrogation room was becoming more and more familiar as Detective Russo and I sat across from each other. My mind went back to the day Bethany died and the last time I was here. I had been on the verge of panic, but not this time. This time, I was pissed.

Detective Russo advised me when I was arrested that I should get an attorney, but what lawyer would believe me if I told them the truth? I had shaken my head when he asked, and I did the same thing when he asked me for a second time in the room. Now, I wished that I had listened to him.

The evidence against me was overwhelming, to say the least. Detective Russo laid the knife that I had pulled out of Ernest on the table, which was also the weapon used to slit Beth's throat. He said the only fingerprints they pulled off the knife were mine. Pair that with finding my phone in Beth's room, me being at both scenes of the crime and having no alibi for either of their deaths, tampering with the crime scene (which, okay, *maybe* I shouldn't have put the stuff I knocked off back, but in my defense, I was in shock), and an anonymous tip the police got to check out the shop while I was in the back room with Ernest's body, and you get the perfect suspect. I was probably going to jail because someone was framing me for these murders. I mean, if I didn't know with absolute certainty that I had nothing to do with their deaths, I would have thought I killed them, too.

Probably going to jail was also a bit of an understatement, considering I wore a neon orange jumpsuit that washed out my complexion and handcuffs that attached to chains wrapped around my waist. They had fingerprinted me when we first walked in too, and I also now had an official mugshot.

I hadn't said a word throughout the entire encounter with Russo because if there's one thing I learned from watching late-night crime shows with Mom, it was to always invoke your right to stay silent.

So, Detective Russo and I just stared at each other. His expression was hard, but his eyes held something that seemed like sympathy. No, that couldn't have been it. It was probably pity. *Poor Ophelia Allan, she went through so much trauma, and she finally snapped.* That's most likely what he was thinking right now.

The cold metal of the handcuffs bit into my right wrist. Detective Russo had to un-cuff one of my hands to attach them to the table. He had re-cuffed my hand too tight, but I wasn't about to give him the satisfaction of speaking first, so I ignored the pain as best I could.

What was harder to ignore was my body's shivering. They once again had the air on in the room, and considering we were now in full-on New England winter mode, I knew it was to make the environment as uncomfortable as possible.

I noticed a slight movement from Detective Russo. Like he, too, was trying to withstand the cold.

He sighed. "What I can't understand is why? Why did you kill these people?"

My lips stayed shut, and I flinched as his fist pounded the table.

"I'm asking you a question! Give me something, Ophelia."

I wanted to. I wanted to shout that I didn't kill my best friend, or that poor, sweet man. But I couldn't. There were too many people wrapped up in Dhazor's scheme, and I hadn't figured out who I could and couldn't trust yet. Even Willow... it was weird how she had gotten a call right before I went inside the shop, but I couldn't prove she had anything to do with it, and after what happened with her parents...

I pushed the thought out of my head. Willow had nothing to do with this. She couldn't have. I didn't think she did anyway. I couldn't analyze any of that right now, though. Not when I faced two murder charges. What would happen to my mom? She had probably heard by now. From someone. Maybe the police had called her. Or maybe no one had called her, and she didn't even know I was in trouble. The only thing worse than her not knowing what was happening to me was for me to put her through more grief so soon.

Seven months. That's how long it had been since...

I closed my eyes, and the chains rattled as I shifted in my seat.

"Ophelia." Detective Russo called my name.

My eyes opened and landed on his gaze. His eyes were wide, his face pleading.

"The cameras are off," he said, "but they'll come back on in exactly one minute, so if you're protecting anyth — any*one*, you need to tell me now. I can help you, but only if you talk to me. Tell me about the carvings in the skin. Give me *something* to go on. Let me help."

A tear escaped down my cheek, but again, I didn't utter a sound. I may not have known who I could trust, but I knew for certain I couldn't trust the guy trying to put me away for the rest of my life.

A few seconds later, the door lurched open, and an officer poked his head in. Detective Russo's lips thinned, and he turned to the officer.

"I'm in the middle of an interrogation." His voice was razor sharp.

"Sorry, detective, but the camera in this room went down, and I had to make sure everyone was okay."

Detective Russo's lips thinned, and he stood, gathering up all the evidence on the table. "We're fine. You can take Miss Allan to her cell, thank you."

He glanced at me and sighed as he shook his head and walked out. The officer who interrupted us hauled me up roughly and led me down a small corridor to a single cell with bars as thick as my forearm. He shoved me inside, and the clang of the metal door shutting was the last thing I remembered before breaking down sobbing.

Chapter Eighteen

For three days, all I could do was lie on the paper-thin mattress of my bunk and stare at the ceiling. There was a tiny window in my cell so I could tell time was passing, but night and day meant nothing to me at the moment. My mind kept replaying every word Ernest had told me, but the more I sat with his words, the harder they were to understand.

"Unless you can stop her acolytes from sacrificing three more innocent souls by the time nature brings new life."

What did that even mean? Who were the acolytes? And who was "her"? I threw my arm over my face and groaned.

I yelped as the cell door clanged open. I sat up and came face to face with Detective Russo, who wore a look of absolute fury on his face.

"If it were up to me," he seethed, "you'd still be rotting in here, but you just made bail. Congratulations."

Confused, I stood up. My arraignment had been that morning, and it was just past noon, judging from the sky outside my window.

Detective Russo escorted me to the front of the building after I changed into some suitable clothes, where Dhazor and my mother were both waiting. I stopped dead. No, I wanted to keep my mother away from all this. Detective Russo raised an eyebrow as my mother rushed over and hugged me so tight, I thought my head might pop off. My arms didn't move to hug my mom back. I was frozen in place as Dhazor just smiled at me. I didn't return the smile.

"Mom." I found my voice, wiggled out of her embrace, and looked at her. Several more wrinkles etched her face, and her hair had more gray in it. How much had I worried her over the past few months? "What are you doing here?"

She smiled gently at me as she brushed some of my ratted hair out of my face. "Your headmaster called and told me what happened. He flew me out first class, and paid your bail as soon as he could. He really cares about his students, doesn't he?"

I could feel Dhazor's eyes on us, so I forced a smile onto my face. "Yes, he does."

My mother tensed as she glanced behind us, then stalked up to Detective Russo and put her finger in his face.

"You should be ashamed of yourself, targeting a teenager. How pathetic can you be?"

Russo just arched his brow. "Be careful, ma'am. I'm still an officer of the law, and I have every right to put *you* in jail if I feel threatened."

She stomped her foot, whirled away from him, and marched toward the door, motioning for me to follow. The three of us made our way out of the station, Detective Russo following. Dhazor paused long enough for me to walk ahead of him, and he put his hand on the small of my back. I fought the urge to physically cringe at the touch. A car was waiting to take us back to the academy, and as I was getting into the back seat, I heard Russo mutter, "I'll be watching you," as he turned and made his way back into the station.

The gates of the academy creaked open as the car rolled onto the property. Panic started to set in, and I couldn't let Dhazor see, so as we stepped out into the cold afternoon air, I headed inside, not waiting for my mom even though the last thing I wanted was for her to be in Dhazor's presence alone. I didn't stop until I was safely inside my dorm.

I flung myself onto my bed and took several deep breaths, trying any and all grounding techniques I could. When that didn't work, I made my way down the hall to the bathroom and splashed my face with cold water. I managed to calm myself down, but only made it halfway back to my dorm before a pair of arms grabbed me. I struggled, but when Dorian's voice broke through my panic, I immediately stopped fighting.

I turned in his arms, and without saying a word, I crushed my lips to his. He let out a surprised groan, but tightened his embrace and deepened the kiss a second later. I grabbed his messy brown hair and pulled him closer. He moved one of his arms from my waist and tangled his fingers in my hair.

Dorian pulled away after a minute, but we were both panting. He laid his forehead against mine and sighed.

"I was so worried," he said.

"So was I."

Dorian kissed me again. This time his lips were gentle, but he pulled away from me completely after.

"My dad has eyes everywhere. We shouldn't have done that so openly."

"Who cares?" I asked. "He knows we're together. Couples kiss."

Dorian looked down at me, his face solemn, and for the first time I noticed his eyes were a dull shade of silver, almost like shining metal that had been worn down over years of exposure. One of his eyes also sported a bruise so deep it looked pure black.

"Who did that to you?" I brushed my fingers lightly over his eye, and he looked away.

"Who do you think?"

I gasped quietly. "Your dad did that?"

He nodded.

I clenched my fists at my sides. "I'm going to kill him."

Dorian shoved his hands in pockets and sighed. "No, you're not. You're going to do what he says. We both are."

My eyebrows knit together. "What do you mean?"

He bit his lip. "Do you know why he brought your mom here?"

I shook my head.

"As... insurance."

My face paled as I let what he was saying sink in. I swallowed hard.

"But... it's my choice."

"Sure, but did you really think he was going to make it easy for you to say no?"

I felt my knees buckle, and I fell to the ground. Dorian stayed where he was, but flinched like he wanted to help me.

Instead, he turned from me.

"I'm sorry." He walked away, leaving me heaving on the ground.

Back in my dorm, I flopped on my bed and cried for the thousandth time that week. I was surprised I was still hydrated enough *to* cry, considering all the tears I shed in that small concrete cell. A knock sounded at my door, and Alisa came in with a bottle of water, as if she knew how much I had been crying. She set it down on the nightstand and knelt so she could be eye level with me.

"You should drink something," she said.

I didn't reach for the bottle.

"Dhazor has invited the Order members who are remaining on campus for the break over to his estate for a dinner tonight," she continued. "Your mother's going."

My eyes shot to hers. They held no warmth, no sympathy, not even happiness. They were... empty.

Alisa shrugged as she held my gaze. "I'm sorry, but I tried to warn you."

She stood up and walked out, shutting the door behind her. I screamed as I chucked a pillow at her, and even though she wasn't there for it to make contact, I felt a little better.

I wiped the snot away and climbed off the bed. Lifting the mattress, I took out two pieces of paper that I kept hidden. One was the yellowed parchment that was on my dresser the night the Order let me in. The other was also a yellowed piece of parchment, but felt older, like it belonged in a museum, rather than stuffed under a bed. I ran my hand over that paper like I had done every night since I ripped it out of Dhazor's compendium.

Mortem Revocare

"Reverse Death." I muttered to myself as I once again unfolded the spell and read the instructions.

I had had no intention of ever actually performing the ritual but having it with me made me feel more in control. Of what, I didn't know, but my life felt like someone else had been making all the decisions ever since the day I walked into my house several months ago.

A faint knock sounded, but it came from the front door. Alisa and someone else were talking, and the voices got slightly louder as they moved into the common area.

I quickly stuffed the two pieces of paper back under the mattress and wiped my face. I took a deep breath and went to see who was here.

Willow smiled when she saw me, and I smiled back. Internally, I melted with relief because I honestly didn't feel like I could handle interacting with someone I didn't know or like. We hugged as Alisa plopped on the couch, flipping her platinum hair and scrolling through her phone.

"I just came to check on you," Willow said.

Perching in the armchair next to Willow, I said, "Thanks, but I'm doing okay." I glanced at Alisa out of the corner of my eye. "I'm excited about tonight's dinner. Is it only the Order that's invited?"

Willow must have also noticed Alisa eavesdropping because she made a show of being uninterested.

"I mean, yes and no," she said. "He does this every year. Dhazor flies the families of the Order members out and hosts a huge holiday party at his estate on the edge of town. This year though, with everything happening, it's just us. Well, us and your mom."

I nodded absentmindedly. Alisa was still staring at her phone, but she wasn't paying attention to it. Instead, her mouth set in a thin line, and she had one of her perfectly shaped eyebrows arched. She *was* eavesdropping.

I turned my attention back to Willow. If Alisa wanted to be Dhazor's spy, that was fine with me. He dragged my mom into this mess. The more he knew I hated him, the better.

"Oh my god," Willow gasped, "We *need* to pick our outfits for tonight! Come on, I'll help you first."

Before I could question the sudden change in tone, Willow rolled to my bedroom, and I reluctantly followed.

Once I closed the door behind us, Willow sagged in her chair.

"Sorry," she said, "I thought Alisa would leave, but she wasn't budging. Here."

She handed me a bright white envelope with the school's letterhead. It looked official. I ripped it open and found a piece of lined notebook paper with almost half the page filled with hastily scrawled words.

Bubbles, I'm sorry for earlier. I didn't mean a single word of what I said, but my father is growing more impatient, or more irritable, that you haven't accepted his offer yet. He's suspicious that I'm the reason, and he brought your mom here to make sure we both comply. We'll have to fly under the radar from now on but know that I will never leave you to face this or any threat that comes our way alone. I could never express my feelings for you clearly, but please know there is no one in any realm that compares to you. You are so exquisite you command the moon and stars to shine brighter. Your bravery and passion light a fire in me I wasn't sure I could ever have. I love you.

Yours in heart and soul, D.

I read and reread the letter, letting those three words sink in. Sitting on the bed, I took several deep breaths. *I love you.* Three simple words that, separately, didn't mean much, but together meant everything. I smiled at the letter as I read it one more time before I folded it, but instead of storing it under the mattress, I folded it more and more until it was a tiny square, and I shoved it in my bra. I turned to Willow, who was scrolling through her phone, obviously trying to give me some privacy.

"So," I asked, "dress code for tonight is what?"

Willow looked up and gave me a wolfish grin as she pulled out a bag from her attached organizer. She tossed it onto the bed next to me.

"I grabbed this for you while we were at the boutique," she said.

I pulled out a neon orange tee shirt and threw it back at her.

"Funny, but the trial isn't until April."

Willow stifled a giggle and pulled out another bag and handed it to me. "Sorry. It was too hard to resist. *This* is the actual outfit I got you."

I pulled out the thin maroon fabric, and at first I thought it was my cloak, but I gasped lightly as I gawked at the dress. The skirt was made with a draped chiffon, and the bodice was a boned corset that laced up in back and shone with hundreds of tiny shimmering crystals.

"It's perfect." I got off the bed and hugged Willow. "Thank you."

"You're welcome," she said, "Let Dorian silently eat his heart out."

Willow wheeled herself toward the door. "We should get changed. Dhazor's personal car is picking us up in two hours, and I have a feeling he's going to try something sneaky tonight, so be ready."

The door clicked shut as I turned toward my mirror and held up the dress.

I felt anything but ready.

Chapter Nineteen

D HAZOR'S MANSION WAS OSTENTATIOUS, to say the least. It was easily the biggest house in the entire town and sat on what looked like acres of land. The white exterior matched the snow on the ground almost perfectly, but he had decorated the exterior in so many strings of soft white lights that there was no mistaking the towering structure.

There were nine of us in total attending the dinner. My mother, seven Order members, including myself, and of course, Dhazor, but only the students had been chauffeured from the academy. My mother was already waiting inside the mansion, according to Alisa.

There were two members attending who I hadn't gotten to know very well over the last few weeks, even though I tried to integrate into the Order as much as I could. Elijah, who made a show of staying away from me, and Gwen — the girl with sharp green eyes and curly black hair that seemed like it had a mind of its own. She and I had spoken three times in total. Once was when she told me to leave Bethany's memorial service. I didn't think either of them liked me very much, and could very well be more of Dhazor's spies.

Someone dressed in a tuxedo opened the double glass front doors and ushered us inside. The interior of the mansion was even more gorgeous than the exterior. Garlands of fresh evergreen branches mixed with more strings of light wrapped around the banisters of the grand staircase and hung across every doorway. It was like someone had copied a picture out of a magazine and pasted it into the house.

Willow laced her arm through mine as we strolled deeper into the estate. She wasn't using her chair tonight since there would be no strenuous walking involved, and she looked gorgeous. Her dress was a long, metallic gold halter dress, and unlike mine, it hugged her curves all the way down her body.

She had her hair pulled up in a tight bun and glittering diamonds hung from her ears.

"He used magic to make it look this good." Willow must have noticed my ogling, and her voice was barely a whisper as we entered a sitting room large enough to house the entire Raven's Cove sophomore class.

My face scrunched into a sneer. Of course, he used magic to get what he wanted. That's what he always did.

"Ophelia, honey, are you feeling okay?"

My mom strolled up to me and Willow with what looked like a martini in her hand. Her cheeks were flushed, and her words slurred slightly. How many drinks had she had?

I nodded and introduced Willow and my mom. Mom looked like she was so happy that I had made a friend. Well, made a friend who hadn't been murdered, anyway. My mother looked as gorgeous as always, with her auburn hair curled to perfection, a few streaks of gray visible among the red. She wore a dark gray pantsuit, and the diamond necklace my dad gave her on their third wedding anniversary rested on her sternum.

The three of us sat down on the paisley sofa. A woman in a sleek black dress offered Mom another cocktail while handing Willow and me champagne glasses full of what smelled like sparkling grape juice.

Dorian was in the corner chatting with Alisa, and she ran her hand down his arm. I had the satisfaction of seeing him jerk away from her touch, though I tried to keep my face as neutral as possible. We caught each other's gaze, and a thousand messages passed between us. A millisecond later, the moment passed as Joel jokingly punched Dorian in the arm and the three of them started another conversation.

Dhazor sauntered into the sitting room looking as young and healthy as ever, and everyone's attention turned to him. Even my mother seemed drawn to his presence. The only people who didn't look enamored were Willow, Dorian, Elijah, and me. I made a mental note to ask Dorian about Elijah's alliances when we were alone.

It took effort not to roll my eyes as Dhazor cleared his throat, even though no one was talking, and began a speech.

"Thank you all so much for coming to my annual holiday soiree. It warms my heart to see so many of my students and their families celebrating here with me tonight."

He nodded toward my mother and me. She beamed back and I forced a grin to my lips.

"Dinner will be served shortly," he continued. "Until then, you can ask the wait staff for any refreshments. Let's make tonight a memorable one, shall we?"

He looked directly at me as he raised his glass, and we all raised ours in return. If what Willow suspected about tonight was true, then I might very well have to choose between keeping my mother safe and becoming *his*, or refusing him, which might cost my mother her life.

Dhazor walked over and held out his hand to my mother. "Mrs. Allan, why don't I give you a tour of the estate? Ophelia can accompany us since she hasn't seen the property before, either."

She took his hand and brushed off her blazer as she put her drink on the side table and rose to her feet.

Dhazor's command for me to follow was clear. I stood a moment later and smiled.

"You're such a gentleman, Headmaster Keswick. And please call me Daisy," Mom said.

Was she... flirting?

I wanted to gag as Dhazor chuckled. "Well then, Daisy, I insist you call me Mathias."

They continued their banter as he showed us the parlor and the back garden, which I hated to admit was gorgeous. Lights were poking out of every crevice of the long evergreen hedges, and even though the stone fountain was off for the season, it too was draped in light.

In fact, so many lights dotted the entire house that you could probably see it from space.

Mom told Dhazor she was cold and huddled up to him, and after a moment of him holding her, and me trying not to gag, he led us back inside and up the grand staircase.

The second floor of the mansion was modest compared to the ground floor. It almost looked like he had never expected to entertain guests upstairs. The blue runners along the marble floor were dull, and the paint on the walls was peeling. In fact, it looked like the upstairs belonged to an entirely different house. My stomach tightened as we ventured deeper.

A loud creak made my head turn, and I saw Mom and Dhazor stepping into the room at the end of the long hallway. I was still near the stairs, and I wasn't aware I had fallen so far behind. I jogged to catch up, and as I entered the room, I saw my mother unconscious on the floor.

"Mom!"

I tried to get to her, but powerful arms yanked me back. Dhazor twisted me to face him, and I gasped. Something deeper than rage filled his features, and staring at his expression, I could understand why no one refused a Divine Demon.

"I've tried being patient with you, Ophelia." His voice slithered down my spine like nails on a chalkboard. "I thought if I gave you time to adjust to the idea, you would see how enticing my offer was and you would come around."

His grip tightened on my arms to the point of pain. "And every time you kissed my *son*, I wanted to kill you both, but again, I waited for you to come to your senses. I can see now that was pointless, and I want my answer. Now."

Even though his grasp was cutting off circulation to my arms, I gritted my teeth as I fought through the deep ache in my bones. I was impressed with myself that I could still manage a look of pure hatred and defiance as I glared dead into the eyes of evil.

"My answer is *no*."

Dhazor emitted a growl so loud it rattled the windows and froze me to my core.

"Then perhaps you need some convincing." He thrust one of his hands out and my mom's shriek pierced the air. I tried to run to her, but Dhazor still had me in a vise grip, and yanked me back so hard, my shoulder screamed in pain.

"Let her go," I pleaded.

Dhazor twisted his free hand, and Mom's shriek turned blood-curdling. I shrank back from the noise and blinked back hot tears.

"Has your answer changed?"

"My lord!"

Dhazor and I whirled toward the doorway where Elijah stood, wide-eyed.

"Give her more time," he begged. "I'm sure she'll come around to your offer. With classes and the stress of being charged with two murders, I'm sure she just hasn't had a lot of time to think about it."

Dhazor glanced between me and Elijah, and his eyes eventually landed on my mother. He pulled me close to his body.

"You have until the end of winter break. Until then, your darling mother stays here with me."

He shoved me away, and I rushed to my mom's side as she stirred.

"What happened?" Her voice was hoarse, but she didn't appear to have any visible injuries.

I helped her into a sitting position as she rubbed her head like she had a migraine.

Dhazor knelt next to us. "I warned you my cocktails were strong, my dear," he chuckled. "You must have had too much to drink. Here, let me help you up."

"How embarrassing." My mother took Dhazor's outstretched hand, and he held most of her weight as we made our way back downstairs.

"Why did you do that?" I whispered to Elijah.

He shushed me but said nothing else. The dinner bell rang right as we reached the landing in the foyer. I'd deal with Elijah later. For now, I just had to get through dinner.

Apparently, no one downstairs had heard the commotion except Elijah and Dorian. Although I was pretty sure Dorian had pretended to ignore it to keep us safe, since his face was pale and he wasn't eating.

Everyone else was laughing and smiling. Willow and Joel were even fighting over who got the last dinner roll. As for my mom, she was sitting beside Dhazor, too close for my comfort, but apparently not enough for hers. She kept sneakily trying to push her chair closer to him, and he smiled at me knowingly.

I didn't eat anything either. My arms screamed in pain every time I lifted them, and even though I didn't have any instant bruises blossoming on my skin, I was sure I would be black and blue later.

I wanted to race out of the room and cry. Watching my mom flirt with anyone was hard, but with a Divine Demon that wanted me to marry him? It made me sick to my stomach.

The man who initially opened the front door for us wheeled in a cart full of beautifully wrapped gifts and set one in front of each Order member.

Dhazor clinked his glass and stood as all the chattering stopped.

"These gifts represent my eternal thanks for everything you all have done, not only for me, but for yourselves, and for everyone around you. I know spending the holidays away from family can be rough, but I would like to think each of you is a part of my family. You all are what makes Raven's Cove Academy the best boarding school on the Eastern Seaboard. To you, my students."

Everyone raised their glass except me. I just stared daggers at Dhazor, and he winked at me as he sipped his drink.

The night thankfully ended soon after, and Dhazor's driver ushered all the Order members back to Dhazor's personal car to be taken back to the academy. Mom waved at me from the open entryway, and Dhazor made a show of winding his arm around her waist. My mom's life was now tied to me accepting a demon's marriage proposal.

As soon as we were inside the academy's gates, I went straight to my room, not bothering to talk to Willow when she asked me what happened. There was only one person I wanted to speak to. The only person I have wanted to see for months. I quickly dressed in a warm long-sleeved thermal shirt, some black fleece leggings, and my brown knee-high boots. I was going to be outside for a while, so I needed to be dressed for the weather. Snatching the yellowed parchment I had ripped out of Dhazor's compendium from under the mattress, I tucked it in my waistband and brushed past Alisa as I made my way to raise the dead.

Chapter Twenty

New England winter during the day was rough. New England winter during the night was absolutely brutal. Even through my warm clothes, the intense cold seeped into my bones. I wrapped my arms around myself as I made my way around the back of the main building toward the edge of campus.

The deep bruises Dhazor had given me groaned in protest with every shiver, and the plastic sack full of the ritual ingredients crinkled. I hadn't needed to refer to the parchment as I grabbed a bag from an unlocked janitor's closet and stuffed it full of everything the spell needed.

The trees soon engulfed me as the lights from the campus disappeared. Snow was scarce under the canopy of trees, and the sack hit a bare patch of dirt with a thud. My fingers were already numb as I lifted several things out of the plastic and started preparing for the ritual. My mind kept wandering back to that horrific day, and for the first time since, I didn't push the memories away.

I thought about the approaching sirens and the flashing lights of first responders as I poured salt in a large circle. The officer who took my statement flashed through my head as I placed ten white emergency candles just outside the salt ring. When everything was ready, I wiped the frozen tears from my cheeks and read the spell as I lit each candle.

"Voco ad animam de Transierunt. Defunctus spiritus conversus ad cinere. Calefacere ossa per lucem flammae. Bibere sanguinem viventium et resurgere."

I had no idea what I was saying, but thankfully the air was still, so every wick burst to life with ease. I didn't know what I expected to happen when I lit the last candle. Maybe a whoosh of light, or a portal opening from the afterlife, but what I didn't expect was for me to stand there in the freezing cold watching a bunch of candles flicker in the dirt.

I groaned and stomped my foot in frustration, snapping a twig. Why wasn't it working? I looked at the parchment again. It was hard to read in the dark, and I had forgotten my phone in the dorm. I knelt by the light of a candle and squinted, trying to make out any words I could, and one word jumped out at me.

Sanguinem. I took one semester of basic Latin back in middle school, but I was pretty sure sanguine meant... blood. I sighed as I got to my feet. Of course, one of Dhazor's spells required blood. I kicked myself for not thinking of that because, like that night down in the basement, there was nothing to draw blood with.

My body shivered again, and I tried to think. Maybe if I had something sharp, that wasn't necessarily metal. I blamed the stress of the night as I realized I was in a forest full of sharp wood, and I got on my knees and felt for the stick I broke. My hands grasped something rough. I picked it up and sure enough, the end of the twig was jagged.

I stood over the circle again and recited the spell one more time while swiping the sharp wood down my palm. Hot liquid pooled in my hand, warming my skin, and I tilted my wrist so the blood dropped in the middle of the circle.

A breeze whistled in my ears, making me draw my arm back into myself for warmth. The wind whipped around me faster and harder until it felt like a tornado was trying to suck me up. I shrieked as the howls of the wind became roars. Deep, guttural sounds that were definitely not human. Despite the cyclone, the candles were still flickering, and in an instant, they erupted upward, the flames almost burning me, making me stumble and fall backward onto the hard ground.

I tried to stand, but the wind held me in place. The growls got louder and closer. Black, shining claws burst from the earth and gripped the dirt. Another set of claws followed. Whatever I summoned, it wasn't human, and it was trying to pull itself into this world. I still couldn't move. All I could do was sit in terror and whimper as four gleaming yellow eyes met mine, and a second later a set of razor-sharp teeth.

Fully emerged, it looked like someone had dipped a greyhound in black motor oil and attached two curly goat's horns to its head.

Smoke poured out of its mouth as it prowled toward me, the stench of rotten meat surging through my nostrils with every gust of piercing wind. The demon dog coiled its hind legs like it was about to pounce. I squeezed my eyes shut and waited for a death that never came.

Instead, I heard a crack and a shrill yelp. I opened my eyes and found Dorian in front of me, facing down the demon dog. His body was taut, ready for anything the demon dog threw at him.

And oh man, that demon dog threw a curveball, because not only did it blow smoke, it breathed fire.

A column of spiraling flame came barreling toward Dorian, but with a flick of his wrist, a plume of shadows erupted in his hand like a living blade. He pointed the blade toward the fire and the darkness swallowed the flames like a black hole. A second later, Dorian rotated his wrist, and the demon dog's body twisted at an unnatural angle with a sickening crunch. He swiveled his wrist again, and the demon dog howled in pain. One more flick of his hand, and the demon's body popped like a balloon, spraying black ooze all over the place, dousing the candles out with a hiss.

The wind died down, but I still couldn't move. I looked at Dorian with wide eyes as he turned toward me. His irises not only glowed with molten silver, but they also burned so brightly they engulfed the whites of his eyes. He knelt in front of me and cocked his head to the side, almost like he didn't recognize me and was sizing up his prey.

"D-Dorian." My voice was hoarse.

He cocked his head to the other side. I licked my lips and tried again.

"Dorian, it's me. It's Ophelia."

"Ophelia," The voice that came from his throat didn't sound like Dorian. It didn't even sound human.

"Bubbles," I said, "remember? Like the Powerpuff Girl."

A crack of thunder overhead made the ground shudder. I flinched at the sound, and Dorian looked up at the sky like he was going to fight it. When he looked back at me, his eyes were their normal shade of silver.

"Bubbles, not like the Powerpuff Girl, but like the carbonation in the soda I offered you the first night we met."

His voice had returned to normal, and I sighed with relief.

Thunder boomed again, and he helped me to my feet. We raced back toward campus as the clouds opened up and rain poured down.

We stopped to take cover in the broken-down greenhouse I had found the key in. It offered us little shelter from the cold, but at least the rain wasn't as bad. A few streams of water still found their way in through the several shattered windows, though. I huddled in a corner of the greenhouse, next to a few large planters. Dorian was still standing, watching for anything that might have followed us from the forest.

"I think we're safe," I muttered through chattering teeth.

Dorian faced me, and his expression was devoid of anything. No anger, no disappointment. His eyes didn't hold the usual spark, either. His entire demeanor was... empty.

I stood up and wrapped my arms around his waist. He didn't hold me back.

"Dorian," I whispered.

He looked down at me. I caressed his face, and I saw the tiniest bit of life come back to him. I kissed his cheek, and he sucked in a deep breath. My mouth moved from his cheek as I pressed a gentle kiss to his mouth. He moved out of my embrace and faced away from me. I wrapped my now-empty arms around myself.

"What's wrong?" I asked.

"What's wrong?" He whirled back around. "What's wrong is that you summoned a demon, Ophelia, and you are damn lucky I caught the scent of it before my father did!"

I flinched back at his outburst, and he pinched the bridge of his nose, taking several deep breaths.

"Why?" he asked. "Why would you do something so reckless?"

Something wet ran down my cheek, and I couldn't tell if it was a stray raindrop or a treasonous tear. It didn't matter either way. I wiped it from my face before Dorian could see. I trudged to one of the wooden tables and hoisted myself onto it, hugging my knees to my chest and listening to the onslaught of the storm. The memories I had kept at bay for months started flashing in my mind, one after the other. The front door swinging open, a scream so devastating I didn't think it was mine, sirens, a gurney that transported the body bag.

I jerked back to reality as Dorian caressed my back in long soothing strokes, and as I took a shaky breath in, I noticed snot had dribbled from my nose. I wiped it away with my sleeve, not knowing when I had started silently sobbing.

"Ophelia." It was only my name, but Dorian said it with so much love and comfort that my heart swelled.

I swiveled my body toward him, my legs dangling off the edge of the table. He was standing next to me, and I was shocked at how tall he actually was. I was used to looking up at him when I was standing, but even with the table giving me extra height,

I still had to lean my head back slightly. I studied his silver eyes, which seemed to glow in the night, and I knew without a doubt that I loved him just as he loved me. And it was time he knew the awful truth.

"It was the last day of my freshman year," I started, "and the school let us out an hour early because someone was smoking in the bathroom and it triggered the fire alarm. My mom was still at work, so my friend's dad gave me a ride home. I remember it being weird that my dad's car was in the driveway, but I just thought that he'd had a short day at work, too. I remember putting my key in the door and..."

I took a shaky breath in as I rubbed my hands together. Dorian took my hands in his and warmed them up with his breath.

"I couldn't understand what I was seeing, and I mean, I saw him... d-dangling over the banister, and I *knew*, but I couldn't... process it. I heard myself screaming, and I wouldn't stop."

A sob burst from my chest.

"The rest is a blur. Police, firetrucks, and an ambulance showed up. An officer was making me tell him what happened, and I didn't know how to explain it. I just knew my dad was dead. A few minutes later, two news crews showed up. The story said something about my dad embezzling money from his job, but it was a lie. He wouldn't do that. I know he wouldn't. He wouldn't just kill himself, either. He was the kindest, happiest person I knew."

I took a deep breath as I finally focused back on the greenhouse and Dorian.

"I just wanted to see my dad."

Dorian wrapped his arms around me and pulled me into him.

"I'm so sorry, Ophelia," he said. "I knew something happened, but..."

Dorian didn't finish his sentence. He just tightened the embrace, and the sobbing started again. All the guilt, grief, and rage came out as tears, and they weren't just directed at the news people who slandered my dad, or the school for letting me go home early, or even my mom who shipped me off to a demonic boarding school instead of helping me deal with his death. The pain and the anger were also directed at my dad.

"He left me. Why did he leave me?" I cried into Dorian's chest. "Why didn't he stay with me?"

Dorian kissed the top of my head. "I don't know, Bubbles. I don't know."

We stayed like that until the tears eventually dried up for good and even after, when the rain was still pouring, and thunder still cracked overhead. We huddled together in a semi-dry corner of the greenhouse and lingered in each other's embrace.

Chapter Twenty-One

I AWOKE THE NEXT day feeling very sore, but also like an immense weight had been lifted. Dorian and I had stayed in the greenhouse cuddling until the storm passed last night. He snuck us in through the back door and, before we left to go our separate ways, he kissed me with so much love it made my head spin.

I could still feel the heat from that kiss on my lips as I got dressed. My upper arms did indeed have deep purple bruises on them in the shape of Dhazor's hands, but I also had some cuts and scrapes from last night's botched ritual. They were all easy to hide, except for the gash on my palm. I didn't want anyone seeing it, especially Alisa or Dhazor, so I put gloves on for the day.

Campus was eerily quiet as I had breakfast in the cafeteria. Dorian was there, but as we had agreed, we didn't even look at each other for more than a second. Willow was gawking at me with concern, but I told her for the hundredth time that morning that I was fine. It wasn't a complete lie, either. Last night had given me some clarity, and I wolfed down the rest of my breakfast before heading to the shuttle stop in front of the school.

Last night's storm had wreaked havoc on the roads, and several of them had completely iced over, but the shuttle rolled up to the academy and picked up me and a couple of other students who were staying on campus. The ride into town felt longer than it actually was, and by the time the shuttle dropped me off on Main Street, my muscles had coiled tight with impatience.

I half jogged, half walked to the small library, careful of the icy patches, and I thought I was doing good at avoiding them until I was almost at the entrance, and my foot slipped out from under me. Flailing my arms frantically, the frozen water won the fight, and I landed on my ass. I shakily stood up and looked around, hoping no one noticed the blunder. When I was satisfied I hadn't embarrassed myself in front of anyone else, I made my way into the warmth of the building.

I had never seen anyone in the library before, and that held true today, too. I still scanned for prying eyes before I unlocked the heavy door in the back and descended the steps.

I grabbed Dhazor's compendium and slammed it down on the table, hoping Dhazor personally felt the blow. Sifting through page after page, I found nothing mentioning acolytes or the symbol that appeared on both Bethany and Ernest. I need-ed Willow's journal and cursed myself for not thinking about bringing it. I plucked my phone out of my pocket to text her, and was disappointed, but not surprised, to find I had no signal. Sighing, I put the book back on the shelf before scaling the steps into the public section of the library.

I almost yelped as my eyes landed on Detective Russo a couple of aisles down, his attention on a book. Was he following me? Had he seen me go into the basement? I tiptoed into the aisle behind him and peeked between the shelves. I squinted so I could see the cover of the book he was reading a little better and had to cover my mouth to muffle the gasp. Detective Russo was reading a book on demons, and from what I could make out, the book was all about the different notable demons throughout the world.

He turned, and I quickly ducked down, hoping he didn't see me. Nothing about this made sense. Was he a follower of Dhazor, or was he trying to gather evidence against me? Both options were possible, if not probable. I stayed crouched as his phone vibrated and he picked it up.

"Are the results in?" he asked.

I couldn't hear the other side of the conversation and I couldn't see Russo's face either, since his back faced me, but the frustrated grunt made me think the "results" were not what he wanted to hear.

"There has to be something connecting them."

Another pause, and Detective Russo sighed.

"Honestly? I know she's involved in all this, and I'm not sure how, but I don't actually see her killing anyone."

A longer pause.

"Doubt it," Detective Russo scoffed. "I'm just hoping putting her on the hook for two homicides will make him show his cards."

My jaw dropped. He was talking about me! Who was "he" though? Did... did Detective Russo know about Dhazor?

"What about the father? Any leads on that?"

Why the hell was he bringing up my dad? I was about to jump up and deck the guy, but what he said made me freeze.

"I never did. The timing was too convenient, and with that embezzlement crap, it was suspicious from the beginning."

A brief pause, and a curt laugh. "The kid's had it rough the past year, and I feel sorry for her, I do, but —"

The person on the other end cut him off. "Right," he said after a moment, "let me know when those results are in."

He didn't say anything else, and after a minute, I heard a book shut and a heavy sigh. Russo's footsteps receded, and I waited a few more minutes before finally unfurling myself. My legs had fallen asleep and would barely hold my weight as I wobbled outside to make a call. When the bitter cold hit me, I was actually grateful.

Twenty minutes later, the academy's shuttle squealed to a halt, and Willow stepped out without her chair. I gave her a big hug as another form stepped down off the shuttle.

Dorian was wearing a thick tan peacoat and a dark brown sweater that almost matched the color of his messy hair perfectly.

I ran toward him and tried to shove him back on the shuttle, but he wasn't budging as the small bus took off.

"What are you doing, Bubbles?" he asked.

I huffed, my breath coming out as a cloud. "You're the one who said we had to be careful and not to be seen together, remember?"

He looked down at me, his eyes gentle. "I believe I also said that I wouldn't let you face any danger alone. I meant what I said."

My hands were still on his chest, and he put one of his own over them. His eyes burned into mine, and I swallowed hard as I subconsciously took a step forward.

"Technically, you wrote it," I whispered.

He smiled, and his hand squeezed both of mine gently.

"And technically, I feel nauseous," Willow said.

I glanced at her and stuck out my tongue. She rolled her eyes and walked into the library.

"You texted me to meet you here so we could do some research, yes?" she called back.

Dorian let go of my hands, and we strolled inside behind her. We went down into the concrete basement, and I moved straight past the compendium and started looking at the other ancient tomes housed on the shelf. I had no idea what I was even looking for, and after a few minutes I went back to the table empty-handed while Dorian was flipping through Willow's journal silently.

"Have you found anything?" I asked.

He shushed me, and I raised an eyebrow.

"Don't worry, he shushed me too," Willow said.

I snickered, and we ended up having a whispered conversation while Dorian read. Occasionally, his face would scrunch up, or he would grunt. I found it adorable while Willow tried not to mock him.

It seemed like hours before Dorian finally put the journal down, and when he did, he just stared at Willow.

"What is it?" she asked, folding her arms on the table.

"You've had this research for years, and you've never said anything about it to anyone."

Willow shrugged. "I don't trust anyone in the Order."

"Even me?" he asked.

"Especially you."

Dorian snorted. "I guess I can respect that. I can certainly understand it, but it would have been really useful to have this earlier."

I snagged the journal off the table and flipped through it. "Have you come across anything about acolytes?"

Willow shook her head and frowned. "Why do you ask?"

I bit my lip. "On Halloween, before I crashed the Order meeting, I wandered into Ernest's shop, and he told me some things."

"What things?" Dorian asked.

His entire body was tense. It didn't even look like he was breathing.

"Something about how I needed to stop 'her acolytes' from making three more sacrifices," I said.

Dorian's eyebrows knitted. "He's human. How would he know about the acolytes?"

He was muttering to himself, and I could see him thinking.

"Well," I said, "I don't think it was Ernest who told me, exactly."

I told Dorian and Willow about how the voice that told me those things didn't sound like Ernest at all. Dorian listened intently and asked follow-up questions, and when I was done, he leaned back in his chair and sighed.

"I knew Ernest was no ordinary human, but how connected he was to the demon realms is unsettling."

"He can do things normal humans can't, but what do you mean 'connected to the demon realms'?" Willow asked.

"You're right, Bubbles," he said, "what you spoke to wasn't Ernest. It was an Auspex, a Leviathan Demon who can divine the future. Divine Demons count on their predictions for a lot of things, and one of an Auspex's abilities is they can also temporarily possess humans."

"That's creepy," Willow said.

I nodded in agreement.

Dorian leaned forward and looked at me so intently I thought I would combust.

"An Auspex's wording is really important, so what *exactly* did it tell you?"

I recited what Ernest/not Ernest told me verbatim, and with each word I said, Dorian's face grew tighter. When I was done, he was silent for a long time. When he finally spoke, his voice was barely audible.

"You should have told me about this earlier."

"I know," I said, "but with Bethany's death, and then Ernest's... I didn't know who to trust."

Willow put her hand on my shoulder and squeezed gently. "I don't think I've ever said how sorry I am about Bethany."

I laid my hand on top of hers and gave her a big smile. "Thank you."

I turned my attention back to Dorian. "What did the Auspex mean when it said 'by the time nature brings new life'?"

Dorian's eyebrows scrunched together. "I'm not sure. An Auspex's words, while important, can have several meanings. My best guess from his words would be the spring equinox."

"That's March twentieth," Willow said, "so we still have some time."

"Not a lot," Dorian said.

I stared at him. "The day after Bethany's death, you said 'it wasn't supposed to happen' and 'they improvised.' Did you know Bethany was going to die?"

Dorian's face widened. "No, I had no idea. When I said that..."

He trailed off and glanced at Willow and then at the table. Willow laced her fingers together and leaned forward, not meeting my eyes.

"The ritual we used for Bethany was different from the ritual you were a part of," she said.

"How so?" I switched my gaze from Willow to Dorian, but neither of them looked at me.

"The normal ritual that you've seen didn't work, so my father took the sacrifice himself." Dorian said.

"He killed her?"

He scoffed. "As much as I would like to say yes, and have the mystery solved, Bethany was alive when he left."

I sighed. "So, if Dhazor didn't kill Bethany, then one of these acolytes did."

Dorian ran his fingers through his hair multiple times.

"Acolytes aren't followers of my dad," Dorian said carefully.

"Then who are they? Because I've never heard of them either." Willow leaned back and crossed her legs.

"I can't say. You two will just have to trust me."

I grabbed Dorian's hands from across the table and kissed them through mine. "I trust you."

Willow scrunched her nose. "I guess I trust you too, but I'm not kissing you."

Dorian chuckled.

I dropped his hands and bit my lip. "There's something else."

Dorian raised an eyebrow, and I explained what I had overheard Detective Russo say on the phone.

"How does your dad fit into all of this?" Willow asked.

I took a deep breath, and for only the second time since it happened, I told the story of his death.

"Shit," Willow said.

"Yeah."

Dorian walked around the table and folded his arms around me.

"It seems like Russo knows more than he's been letting on," he said.

Even in Dorian's embrace, my body was still tense. I leaned my head up and closed my eyes as he kissed my forehead. When I opened them, the only thing I was tense about was still feeling like we were missing something.

Willow stretched out her legs and positioned her body toward us.

"Well, you've already been indicted for murder, right?" she asked. "I say we add kidnapping to that list and make this detective give us answers."

Dorian stood at his full height and crossed his arms while I looked at her with an open mouth.

"Kidding." Willow held up her hands in a surrendering gesture. "Sort of."

Dorian sighed. "I agree we need to determine exactly what he knows, but if Russo *is* involved, we need time to think about our next move."

My stomach gurgled, and Willow busted out laughing. "I think your girlfriend agrees with you."

Being called Dorian's girlfriend made my stomach do flips, and I felt heat rush to my face. Dorian kissed my cheek and I smiled. I stretched as I stood and the three of us headed back to the Academy for food.

Chapter Twenty-Two

D ORIAN, WILLOW, AND I spent the next few days planning how we were going to get Detective Russo to cooperate, changing the plan, and changing it again. It turned out none of us could agree on how to get the information we needed from Russo, and the end of winter break was closing in. I had only heard from my mom a couple of times since the dinner, and each time, I could hear Dhazor in the background. You'd think as headmaster of a school, he would be here doing whatever headmasters did. Instead, he was holding my mother hostage in a mansion.

"Odion might know how we could get to Russo," Willow suggested as she, Dorian, and I lounged in the common room of her dorm one afternoon.

"I've called him, but he's not answering." Dorian pulled out his phone to check again.

I sat in one of the forest green armchairs by the fireplace, watching the flames flicker. It reminded me of the demon dog I summoned, but thinking of that night didn't scare me. No, what scared me was the thought of Dhazor wining and dining my mother.

"Bubbles?" Dorian waved his hand in front of my face, trying to get my attention.

I blinked rapidly and turned toward him and Willow. "Huh?"

Dorian perched himself on the arm of the chair, his lips turned down. "Are you okay?"

I tried to smile and nod, but I could tell neither of them believed me, so I brushed my hair over my shoulder and told them the truth.

"No," I said, "I'm not okay. The end of winter break is in two days, and I still don't have an answer for Dhazor."

"Your answer is no," Dorian said flatly.

I rolled my eyes. "Of course it's 'no,' but as long as he's holding my mom, my hands are tied. And aren't you the one who told me I needed to make Dhazor think I was interested?"

"That was before —" Dorian cut himself off.

"Before what?" I asked.

He threw a glance at Willow and sighed. "Before I knew I loved you."

Dorian's hands clenched into fists as Willow retched. He shot her a glare, and she shrugged, before turning his attention back to me.

"We'll figure a way out of it," he said, "I promise."

I couldn't listen to another "we will" or "what if." I bounced out of the chair and strode for the door. Dorian followed me, but I held a hand up. "I just need to be alone."

"Be careful," he said.

I grunted in response as I walked out the door.

I meandered the halls of the nearly empty campus, trying to think of solutions to any of the problems that had started since I arrived at Raven's Cove Academy, but the warm mahogany of the walls felt too suffocating, so I left the building, and pulled my coat tight around my body. Snow was falling heavily, and the gray clouds were an ominous shade of dark gray.

The ground crunched underneath my feet, and each step I took left deep imprints of my boots. I took deep breaths in and deep breaths out as I looked at the pure white landscape surrounding me.

The sky darkened, and it looked as if night was falling, but when I checked the time on my phone, that couldn't have been it. It was only 3:30 p.m. My feet moved more rapidly, and I paused. The darkness was moving with me.

I rolled my eyes and huffed. "You're a coward, Dhazor," I called. "Come on out."

I didn't scream or raise my voice. I didn't have to. He was there, watching me. Following me.

The surrounding darkness condensed and swirled into a moving shadow that almost held the figure of a person, but not quite. The heavy snowfall also didn't help, and it was a wonder I could barely make out any distinguishable shape.

"My dearest Ophelia." Dhazor's voice sounded like it came from far away, and enveloped me at the same time.

"What do you want?" My voice dripped with so much venom it surprised me.

Dhazor only chuckled. "The same thing I've wanted since the beginning. You."

"I have two days left," I reminded him.

He disappeared, and a second later, he materialized, and not in his shadow form, either. I watched as the shadows swirled tighter together, forming skin and bone, becoming fully corporeal until Dhazor himself stood mere inches from me. He leaned down until his lips were brushing my ear. I wanted to cringe away from him and gag, but I stood my ground.

"You're acting so brave." His breath tickled me, making my stomach churn. "But your heartbeat betrays you. You're scared. But what could you be so afraid of? Are you frightened of what you feel for me?"

I gritted my teeth and straightened my spine, but said nothing. I just stared dead ahead into the intertwined branches of the dormant trees lining the forest.

Dhazor backed up, and I let myself relax, but only slightly.

He shoved his hands in his pockets and let out a breath. "I'm aware you have two days left, but I'm getting impatient, and I do... impulsive things when I get impatient, Ophelia."

I took one deliberate step forward. "If you hurt my mother —"

He took a hand out of his pocket and waved it in the air. My mouth fell silent, and no matter how much I tried, I couldn't utter a sound. Screw magic.

"Yes, yes, if I hurt your precious mother, there will be hell to pay. Is that the threat you were about to make?"

With a slight flick of his wrist, I could talk again.

"Is this how you woo every woman you're interested in?"

Dhazor shrugged. "It's how I won my son's mother, although she didn't fight back as much as you did. In fact, you, Ophelia Allan, are the first one to resist me so thoroughly."

I felt bile rising in my throat. "I take that as a compliment."

The smile forming on Dhazor's face made my blood run cold. His form shifted back into shadows, and the last thing I heard him whisper was, "Tick, tock."

And then he was gone. I was getting really tired of his cat-and-mouse game. And yeah, I'll admit it, I was scared. Really freaking scared. He wasn't going to stop until I gave him the answer he wanted. But I was more pissed off than I was afraid, and something my dad had always told me came flooding back.

A person's future is like a city, there are many buildings with different functions, and they all work together to keep the city alive and thriving. Each building in your city is a part of who you are, Ophelia, and only you can construct it the way you want. Never let anyone else decide how your city is built.

With his words running through my head on repeat, I knew what I had to do. I stomped through the heavy snow and didn't glance back as I left the academy grounds.

I stood in front of Ashton's police station, the snow nearly blinding me as the wind whipped it into my face. I hadn't taken the shuttle because I honestly didn't know if Dhazor would catch wind of where I was going. It wasn't like I truly cared if he knew, but no one else needed to die. Especially not when that person could help me find Beth's killer and, *hopefully*, help me end Dhazor for good.

I squeezed my eyes shut, took one more deep breath, and made my feet move forward.

"Miss Allan?"

I whirled around to find Detective Russo stepping out of a beat-up silver sedan. His demeanor was guarded as I walked up to him. A gust of wind blew, and I shivered, wrapping my arms around me, but I stared at the detective's face, his deep brown skin wrinkled as his expression changed to concern.

"I need your help," I said.

"Okay. We can talk inside." He waved me toward the door of the station, obviously confused about why I would voluntarily come back here.

I huffed. "I know you know about Dhazor."

I wasn't actually 100% certain of that fact, and was taking an enormous gamble, but the complete shock on his face told me I had been right to take that chance.

Detective Russo swallowed and glanced around, presumably to see if anyone was watching, then motioned for me to get in the car. I complied, grateful to be out of the cold and snow. He climbed into the driver's seat and turned on the ignition. Hot air immediately blasted me in the face, and I settled in as Detective Russo pulled out of the station's parking lot.

We drove for fifteen minutes in silence before coming to a stop at a small house with peeling white paint and aged wooden shutters. One of them looked like it was hanging on by a single nail as it swung in the wind, and I started to think getting in the car with a strange man wasn't my smartest move.

Once inside, though, Detective Russo pulled out a chair at the kitchen table for me and heated a kettle on the stove.

"You like tea, right?" he asked.

"Mm-hmm."

Russo disappeared into another room. My leg bounced at a thousand miles an hour, while my eyes glanced everywhere and my teeth dug into my bottom lip. The entire house looked like it was the set of a horror movie. Yellow floral wallpaper peeled at the edges in the living room, and the furniture had holes with white stuffing showing through. Rust ate through parts of the appliances in the kitchen, and knobs were missing from the stove. I tried to take a calming breath, but the smell of old cigarettes and must rushed into my nostrils.

Detective Russo returned and plopped a thick folder in front of me with pieces of paper sticking out, and scooted out a chair across from me.

"This," he said, interlacing his fingers on the table, "is everything I have on Dhazor, or how he's known here, Headmaster Mathias Keswick. As you can see, it's a lot."

I opened the folder with shaky fingers. Inside were newspaper clippings from articles going back several decades, photos, missing person's reports, and...

I slammed the folder shut and looked at Detective Russo with watery eyes.

"Detective —"

He held up a hand. "You're in my home. I think we're past formalities, don't you? Call me Zach."

"*Zach*, my dad committed suicide, so I'm not sure why he would be in a file of demonic shit. Are you trying to get me to, I don't know, confess to something?"

Zach looked at me with sympathy. Like he had probably done to so many victims' families.

"Don't you think it's kind of a strange coincidence that your mom sent you here right after your father died?"

I shook my head as my lips quivered. No. He was not saying what I thought he was. Tears welled up and threatened to fall.

Zachary looked down at his hands and shifted in his seat. "My wife attended Raven's Cove Academy. She was a member of the Divine Order."

He said the Order's name with a mixture of disgust and like it was the most ridiculous name ever, but he didn't stop talking.

"She was a currency member, and she told me she hated every second. Her senior year, she dropped out and left Ashton. When we met, she was skittish, looking over her shoulder everywhere we went. Something had scared her, and the night I proposed, she told me about Dhazor and how he was furious that she left. My wife never felt safe, and she was right to be afraid. In retaliation for leaving, Dhazor killed her father, and eventually, after he was done screwing with her head, he killed her, too."

"I'm sorry for what happened," I said, "but that doesn't mean Dhazor murdered my dad."

Zachary closed his eyes and sniffled. "You're right, it doesn't. But maybe this does."

He took the folder and flipped through several pieces of paper before pulling out a newspaper clipping of a group photo.

I inspected it closely, confused about how it would prove anything, and my mouth fell open. It was a group photo of Order members from several years ago, and standing directly beside Dhazor, beaming, was my mother.

Chapter Twenty-Three

I STARED AT THE photo until my eyes were bleary. It didn't make any sense. Why would Dhazor kill my dad if my mom was a member of the Order? And why was he so hell-bent (no pun intended) on claiming me? My head swam as I sipped the tea Zachary put in front of me. I hadn't even noticed the kettle whistle, but the steaming liquid warmed my bones.

Zachary closed the file and took it from me. He sat back down and crossed his arms on top of the folder.

"Trust me," he said, "if you look for answers in words and pictures long enough, you'll drive yourself mad."

"I refuse to believe it," I sniffled. "My dad had a lot going on, and that's it. He didn't... he wasn't..."

I quickly wiped my cheeks. Zachary had a look on his face. Sympathy, maybe. Or pity. I didn't want to be pitied.

Zachary sighed. "You asked for my help, but if you truly want it, cooperate with me. I'm not asking you to believe what I told you about your dad. You might be right, he might have just been in unbearable pain, but I've spent years studying Dhazor and his patterns. You and your parents fit that pattern, but Bethany and Ernest don't. I know Dhazor has something to do with their deaths, but I haven't been able to figure out how, and I think you know more than you're telling me."

He was asking too much and giving almost nothing of importance away. I crossed my arms and took a deep breath as I leaned back in the rickety chair, hoping my demeanor came off less shocked and more nonchalant.

"How about we cooperate with each other?" I asked.

Zachary raised an eyebrow. "What do you mean?"

My eyes wandered around the room. "Oh nothing, really. I just know you were talking on the phone with someone the other day, and it seems rude to not share the conversation with the class. I mean, as long as we're helping each other."

His lips thinned. "How do you know about that?"

I shrugged. "Alright, you win," he said.

I leaned forward again, and the wood of the chair groaned under the weight.

"I have a friend who works in a lab in Hartford," Zachary explained. "I sent the murder weapon over to him, and he found something that... got overlooked here."

I choked on a laugh. "You mean that you all missed?"

He narrowed his eyes, but continued. "I mean something that was covered up. There was a tiny drop of dried blood between the hilt and the blade of the knife. It was too old to be Mr. Elrod's, and it doesn't match your blood type or Bethany's."

My mouth popped open. "Did you discover this mystery blood before or after you arrested me?"

Zachary shifted in his seat. "After, but I was still going to charge you because —"

"Because it would piss Dhazor off."

"Yes."

My jaw clenched. "So I was bait?"

"Yes."

I took a cleansing breath, consciously relaxing my tense muscles.

"And the results still aren't in?"

Zachary shifted again, drumming his fingers on the table. He was obviously trying to figure out how much to share with me. The ticking of the clock on the living room wall was the only sound for a while.

"No," he finally said. "The results have been delayed, and I think I've shared more than enough for the time being. Your turn."

"Bethany and Ernest's deaths have something to do with 'her acolytes,' but I don't know who 'her' is, and I don't know who these acolytes are, either."

Zachary rubbed his chin. "I've never heard of them, so they don't follow Dhazor."

My phone pinged before I could say anything else. Dorian's name flashed across the screen.

Are you ok? You disappeared hours ago. I'm worried.

I sent a quick text back, letting him know I was fine as I stood and stretched my legs. "I need to get back to the Academy."

Zachary stood as well and took both of our cups to the sink. "I'll give you a ride, but I think it would be best if I dropped you somewhere other than the school."

I agreed as we headed back out into the snow.

Zachary dropped me about a block away from the front gates of the academy. The snow had gotten significantly deeper, and I couldn't see the sidewalk at all as I trudged toward campus. I had gotten through the creaky gates when I heard a shrill scream to my left. I ran as fast as I could toward the sound, which wasn't very fast with the snow, and found a student, who had apparently come back from winter break early judging by her suitcase beside her, kneeling in the snow.

Crimson snow.

Hesitantly, I looked over the student's shoulder. Lying dead in the snow was a boy around our age. He had light ginger hair that was spattered with dark red. Just like Bethany and Ernest, someone had slashed his throat, but he also had a deep gash in his abdomen, and through all the blood I could see bits and pieces of his intestines.

The girl still knelt in the snow, screaming for help. She was rocking herself back and forth as if doing that would make the nightmare scene in front of her go away.

Several faculty members arrived, and a couple led me and the girl inside, while another was on the phone, presumably with the police, but they could have also been talking to Dhazor for all I knew.

The girl and I sat in Dhazor's office, wrapped in blankets. She was still rocking back and forth and sobbing.

"What's your name?" I asked her.

She sniffled. "Kora. Yours?"

"Ophelia."

She didn't say anything else, so I tried talking again.

"Where did you go for break?"

I didn't really care about the answer, but if talking got her mind off the boy's body, I'd be happy to pretend like I did.

She started talking, slowly at first, but when her rocking stopped and her shoulders slumped, she started talking more.

Even through her tear-stained face, I could tell she had been somewhere sunny. Her skin had a glow to it, like she had spent every day of winter break tanning. It made her green eyes pop. Her hair was almost the same sandy shade as mine, but it was chopped short and had perfectly placed highlights.

She was droning on about some boy she met when the door flung open behind us, and in strode Dhazor, and behind him...

Detective Zachary Russo, his face neutral and all business. How could he be so close to Dhazor without showing any sort of emotion? I could barely keep the sneer off my face as he addressed me. I faced him, and his eyes held nothing but pretend compassion, while I'm fairly sure mine held nothing but contempt.

Dhazor asked me what happened, completely ignoring Kora. I gave short answers to every inquiry. Detective Russo stood in the corner of the room, taking notes and asking follow-up questions as necessary, but at least he was including Kora in the conversation.

When all questions had been answered, and Kora was nodding in and out of sleep, Dhazor dismissed us. I caught Russo's eye, and he subtly shook his head. Don't interact with me, he seemed to say.

I was on my way to my dorm when a hand snaked out and grabbed my upper arm. I yelped, and another hand clapped over my mouth.

"Shh." Dorian's voice was in my ear. "Go to your dorm. Tell Alisa you're fine and that you need a shower. Meet me in my room in ten minutes."

I nodded, but when I looked behind me, he was gone. I did as he said and grabbed the neon pink shower caddy my mom had bought me from my room as I assured Alisa I was fine. Once the coast was clear, I sprinted to the other side of the building to Dorian's dorm.

I opened the door without knocking and dropped the shower caddy as I yelled and covered my eyes. Joel and Gwen were on the couch, half naked. I heard them scramble to put clothes back on, and only when I felt someone brush past me on their way out did I open my eyes.

"Do you not know how to knock?" Joel growled.

I scoffed. "Do you not know how to get a room?"

Joel bounced off the couch and strode toward me, his hands in his pockets. He stopped a few feet from me and leaned down.

"This is a room," he said, "and I'm betting you're just jealous because dear Dorian never ravished you like that."

I took a step back and held up my hand, warding him off. "First off," I said, "ew. Second, this is the *common* area, you know, an area that everybody uses."

"Yeah, and I was using it. This isn't even your dorm, so go away."

He made a shooing motion with his hands, and I about smacked him.

Dorian's bedroom door opened, and he leaned against the frame.

"There's another point to be made, Joel," he said. "How do you know I've never ravished her like that?"

"Can we please stop using that word?" I begged.

Joel laughed as he leaned away from me and sat back on the couch. Note to self: spray the couch with Lysol before I sit there again. Dorian chuckled as he pushed himself away from the door frame and sauntered toward me. I picked up my fallen shower caddy and jumped a little when I stood back up to see Dorian inches from me.

He slung his arm around my shoulder and guided me toward an armchair. Dorian sat down first, pulling me onto his lap. I placed the caddy next to us, and Dorian tried to hide a smile.

"Why are you laughing?" I asked.

"I just never thought you'd be into pink."

My face heated. "And what's wrong with pink?"

Dorian's chest rumbled underneath me as he laughed. "Nothing." He brushed some hair over my shoulder and gently pressed his lips at the base of my neck. "It was just a surprise, that's all."

Another kiss, and I leaned my head back.

"I get it!" Joel screamed from the couch.

Dorian laughed as he placed one more kiss on my neck and faced Joel. "At least I don't have her naked on the couch."

"It might do both of you some good," Joel grumbled as he reached for the TV remote.

The TV flickered to life, and Joel flipped through channels until an exterior shot of the school made him pause. It was a news segment about the ginger boy we found in the snow, and the reporter was interviewing Kora about what happened.

"Who's that?" Joel asked.

I shrugged. "She said her name was Kora. I guess she came back from break early when she... found the body."

Dorian tensed underneath me. I adjusted my body so I could face him. "What is it?"

"I don't recognize that student," he said.

"Maybe she just slipped your memory," I suggested. "I mean, you can't memorize the face of every person in the school."

Dorian shook his head, his face scrunched into a deep frown. "No, I'm sure I've never seen her. Kora doesn't attend Raven's Cove Academy."

I turned back to the TV as Kora was wiping away a tear. If she wasn't a student, then who was she?

Chapter Twenty-Four

I TOSSED AND TURNED that night, thinking about Bethany and Ernest, and now that ginger boy lying dead in the snow. I didn't even know his name. And who was Kora? Dorian said she wasn't a student, but from what she'd told me in the office, that wasn't true. And who were the acolytes?

Groaning, I threw my pillow across the room and tossed back the covers. I wandered toward the bench nestled in a small nook and I pulled my knees up to my chest as I watched the snow fall gently outside. It had to have been after midnight, which meant in less than twenty-four hours, I would have to give Dhazor my answer. I had less than twenty-four hours to figure a way out of this mess. Which mess, I wasn't sure, but I needed a solution. I needed answers.

I shook my head as I groaned again. I wasn't going to get answers just sitting here, so I got dressed in thermal clothes and made my way down to the catacombs underneath the school, hoping that one of the winding halls and vast rooms would give me something.

Only there were already people there when I walked toward the main chamber. I hid behind a stone column leading toward the stairs as Dhazor and Kora stared each other down. Dhazor's eyes were ablaze with fury and literal fire.

I couldn't see Kora's full expression, but it looked as if she were smiling.

"You should leave," Dhazor said.

I had heard Dorian's voice when he was angry and trying to keep the demon side of himself in control. It had sounded inhuman, but the weight of Dhazor's full demonic voice chilled me to the core. I thought he was talking to me, but Kora just chuckled.

"I don't think so. My lady sent me here to make sure things were on track, and I intend to do just that."

Dhazor growled, and it shook the entire cavern. "She and her *acolytes* are not welcome in my domain. Leave."

My eyes widened. Dhazor knew who the acolytes were.

Kora clicked her tongue. "This middle of nowhere town is your domain? How the mighty have fallen."

Another growl.

She held up her hands. "Didn't she used to tell you to mind your temper?"

"Get out!" Dhazor roared, the cavern shaking so hard, I had to adjust my footing so I didn't fall.

Kora shrugged and headed toward the ramp that led back to the basement.

"Be careful, Dhazie, or she might just make you her first sacrifice," she called back.

Her footsteps receded, but I didn't hear Dhazor move.

A minute passed. Two.

"You can come on out now." Dhazor still sounded pissed, but also... tired.

I hesitantly walked down the stairs and saw him sitting on the stone ledge in front of the fire. His arms were resting on his thighs and his head sagged. He seemed almost defeated.

"Who —" I started.

"None of your concern." His voice still sounded completely demonic.

I froze, my heart thundering in my chest. If I could just make it to the basement...

"Don't even think about running." Dhazor stood and prowled toward me.

My breathing stopped as he towered over me. Literal fire filled his eyes, and the flames radiated rage. When his hand grazed my cheek, however, it was gentler than I thought he was capable of. My stomach roiled, and it took all my willpower not to flinch away from his touch.

I need my mother safe. I need my mother safe.

He dropped his hand, and I stepped back, putting as much distance between him and me as possible. His eyes shut, and he took several deep breaths. When they opened again, the fire was gone.

"It's the last day of winter break," he said. "What's your answer?"

Wha-what? "I have until the end of today to give you an answer."

Dhazor chuckled darkly. "I said you had until the end of winter break, but I never gave a time. I'll ask once more. Are you willing to be mine, or is your dear mother going to pay the price for your refusal?"

My stomach dropped. There was no answer to give. I had more time. I thought I had more time.

My breathing quickened, and the room spun. Dorian. I loved Dorian. My knees gave out, and I fell to the rocky ground with a hard thump, but the pain barely registered. I wished Dorian were here. Or Willow, or Odion, or anyone who could save me.

Dhazor didn't move to help me. He just stared at me, waiting. Time. I needed more time, and if I couldn't buy myself a few more hours to answer him, I would have to buy time another way.

"I —" My voice was barely audible. I cleared my throat and tried to speak again. "I have a few conditions."

Dhazor's eyes widened, and he laughed. "And what, pray tell, are your 'conditions'? It's not like you have any bargaining power, but I'll humor you."

He sat back down on the ledge, his earlier demeanor forgotten. Dhazor now sat tall with one leg crossed over the other, his head cocked to the side as if a small child were doing something endearing. That's all I was to him. I was a child playing a game he thought he'd already won. That's all any of us were to him.

My anger squelched the overwhelming terror. There was no one here to save me, and I didn't need anyone to save me. I had the power to save myself. I had my own fire, and while it might not physically manifest as flaming eyes, or shadow blades, I had more power over my life than some damned demon.

I got to my feet, and my legs were steady. I tossed my hair over my shoulders and stared Dhazor down. There was only one way out of this cavern, but Dhazor hadn't won anything. In fact, claiming me was his biggest mistake in his game, because I would be his downfall.

My voice was even when I spoke. "My conditions are as follows." I held up my pointer finger. "One, you will immediately release my mother and return her home unharmed." Another finger went up. "Two, I want answers, *honest* answers to any and all of my questions whenever I ask them."

Dhazor gave an amused smirk as I put up another finger.

"Three, I'm sixteen, you sicko. You want me to be yours, you wait until I graduate. And four" — one more finger — "you won't harm Dorian in any way, shape, or form."

Dhazor crossed his arms. "Anything else?"

"Yes," I said, "did you murder my father?"

"No, but since we haven't agreed to anything, you won't know if my answer is honest, will you?"

I strode up to him and let my hand fall. "If you agree to my conditions, I'll agree to yours."

Dhazor's eyes swirled with color and shadow, all melding together like a kaleidoscope of demonic energy. He stood and placed one hand on my cheek and the other on the side of my neck where a burning sensation started. Pain seared my body, and I wanted to collapse, but Dhazor held me upright. Once the pain subsided, he let go, and I fell to my knees, grasping the spot where the pain had originated.

I brushed my skin and gasped as I felt raised skin in the same X shape as on the cover of his compendium. Dhazor had branded his sigil into the left side of my neck.

Dhazor helped me to my feet. "Careful, my dear, the claiming process can be disorienting."

He calls pure agony "disorienting"? I'd hate to experience his idea of pain. Dhazor let me go once I was steady and strolled up the stairs.

He whirled back toward me when he was halfway to the top. "I almost forgot. No, I did not murder your father, however, his death was tragic. I truly hoped your mother had found happiness after what she had done, but I guess some secrets are too heavy. Oh well, I'll be anxiously waiting for your graduation."

He melted into shadows, leaving me alone in the cavern.

Well, shit.

The walk back to my dorm was even more excruciating than the brand. What had Mom done that was so horrible it caused my dad to... I tried to shake the thought from my mind. I had bigger things to worry about right now. Dorian was going to be pissed at the outcome of tonight's events. I just hoped he wouldn't be pissed off at me. At least I could now use Dhazor to my advantage. He had promised me honesty, and I intended to hold him to that promise.

I was so deep in thought that I didn't notice someone was walking down the hallway until I smacked straight into them. I glanced up at Odion's smiling face.

"Hey Allan," he said, "didn't realize I had become invisible during break."

I beamed back, not realizing how much I had missed him until that moment. "Of course you aren't invisible! I just wasn't watching where I was going."

Odion's smile vanished. "Is something wrong?"

I shook my head but tried to keep my hair in front of my face.

"Okay," he said, "it's pretty late, and I have to get unpacked, but we'll catch up later, and you can tell me every embarrassing thing D did when I wasn't here."

He smiled and gave me a dramatic wink. I beamed back, and his face fell as he gawked.

"Ophelia, what in hell did you do?"

"What do you —"

I gasped as I clapped my hand to my neck. I hadn't realized I had tossed my hair out of my face, but it was too late. Odion had seen the brand and knew what it meant.

I didn't know what to say, so I said the only thing I could. "I didn't have a choice."

He threw his head back and barked out a single laugh. When he looked back at me, his eyes were cold.

"You *always* have a choice, and I'll be sure to let Dorian know yours."

He snatched his suitcase and stalked off before I could explain anything else. I took a deep breath, but it did nothing to relax me. Yelling at nothing, I headed back toward the dorm, but Alisa was the last person I wanted to see right now. She idolized Dhazor, and I'm pretty sure she would either squeal in delight or kill me where I stood. Dorian... what would he think? He knew the situation, but he also didn't want his dad anywhere near me. I blinked back tears. There was a way out of this. There had to be, but I was so tired I couldn't think straight.

So, knowing I couldn't do anything at the moment, and having nowhere else to go, I crept back to my room, grateful when all the lights were off. I crawled into bed, the plush covers enveloping me like a cloud, and I fell into unconsciousness.

SPRING

Chapter Twenty-Five

WEEKS PASSED, AND WHILE snow was still on the ground, trees flowered and birds started chirping with the promise of spring. The entire Order knew I had agreed to Dhazor, and also knew that Dorian and I were no longer together. We hadn't officially broken up, but the brand on my neck, and the fight that ensued, sort of did that for us.

He had banged on my bedroom door the morning after I had given Dhazor my answer and I could only describe what followed as a full-on meltdown. We screamed at each other, and I'm pretty sure I saw his shadow blades try to materialize in his fists. I knew he would never physically hurt me, but seeing the blades still made me nervous. He had noticed and worked to calm himself down, but the hurt in his eyes at what I had promised his dad was still as clear as day.

We had talked only a few times since, and each time it had been about Order business. I threw myself into being a productive member, as well as focusing on my schoolwork. My grades were still slipping, however. The Order had done only one sacrifice since coming back from break, too, and I was so numbed by everything that I didn't even flinch when their screaming filled my ears.

Dhazor hadn't bothered to make any more threats, and why would he? He got what he wanted. At night, though, two nightmares plagued me, playing over and over in my head. Dorian's shattered expression when I broke his heart, and the deaths of Bethany, Ernest, and the red-headed boy I had learned was named Jason. Each of their throats slit, with the same sigil carved in each of their palms.

I woke in a cold sweat one night, my fingers grazing the left side of my neck, as if Dhazor's sigil branded into my skin was causing the dreams. Throwing off the damp covers, I padded to the bathroom to splash my face with cold water. I gasped when a woman with pale skin, straight, waist-length brunette hair, and eyes so black, it sparked pure terror, appeared in the mirror behind me. No one was standing behind me when I looked, however. Sucking air into my lungs, I tried to calm my racing heart. I seriously needed sleep.

The next few days, I jumped at every little noise as dark circles clung under my eyes. I could barely keep myself awake enough to make it through even the most interesting class. I got sympathetic looks at the monthly Order meeting. Even Dorian seemed worried, but every time I glanced at him, his eyes would dart away.

Willow rolled up to me after the meeting came to a close. She was as mad at me about Dhazor as Dorian was, and I didn't blame her, but she stared at me with nothing but concern.

"What?" I snapped.

"Is he doing this to you?" Her voice was gentle, like she was comforting a spooked animal.

I sighed. "No... I don't know... I mean, I don't think so."

My thoughts were so jumbled, I couldn't form a coherent sentence. She motioned for me to follow her, and she led me down a corridor I hadn't yet explored. A few minutes passed, and the pathway changed. It was carved out of the same stone as the main chamber, and the sacrifice room, but it seemed older somehow. Like someone had built the main chamber as an addition to wherever we were headed.

Willow made a sharp right turn, and I almost slammed into her trying to follow. The cavern we entered was definitely not part of the catacombs I was used to. The stone was smoother and a lighter shade than the main chamber. Lit torches hung on the walls, illuminating the space enough for me to barely see a large circle carved into the floor. Five smaller circular divots, made for candles to sit in judging by the dried wax, surrounded the main circle at specific positions. In the middle of the large circle was the same sigil that had been carved into the hand of each person who died.

"Where are we?" I asked.

"I don't know."

She took out her journal from the storage bag on the back of her wheelchair and flipped it open. "I've explored all the catacombs during my research, but this was never here. And look." She pointed to the far wall where four glittering obsidian bowls sat on marble pedestals.

I don't know how I missed them, but I treaded over to the bowls, careful to step around the markings on the floor. Dark, viscous liquid filled three of the bowls. I dipped the tip of my finger into the liquid and rubbed the substance between my thumb and pointer finger. Blood. Why did it always have to be blood? My gaze went from the bowls to the carved circle and back. Five divots in the floor, four bowls, and three of them filled with blood.

My heart stopped. I backed away slowly, not daring to take my eyes off the bowls for a second.

"What is it?" Willow asked.

I showed her my hand with the blood on it as if that were explanation enough. I tried to breathe and form words, but neither happened. Willow seemed to understand that whatever I found freaked me out, though, so we turned around and left the catacombs altogether.

We were sitting in her bedroom an hour later, and I had finally found the words to speak again. She sat cross-legged on her bed, and I slouched forward in her desk chair, exhaustion washing over my entire being.

"We've been missing something huge," I said, "and looking in that room finally made it click."

"Made what click?" Willow asked as she leaned over and grabbed a bag of cheese puffs from her bedside table. My nose crinkled.

"Everything. When you first showed me your journal, you said students died. How many died?"

"Three," Willow said as she took a cheese puff and popped it into her mouth.

I tugged on a strand of my hair. "And each one had the same sigil on their hand?"

She nodded. "I didn't actually see the sigils myself, but I saw a photo in the town paper, and the sigil looked blurry."

I rubbed my temples. "Blurry?"

Another crunch. "Like the camera shook while taking the picture, but it was weird because the rest of the photo was sharp."

I straightened in my chair. "Can I borrow your journal for a bit?"

Willow's hand that was rummaging around in the foil bag stilled. "Why?"

"Because I don't think that was camera shake. Remember what the Auspex said? 'Stop her acolytes from sacrificing three more innocent souls by the time nature brings new life'. The three students who died a couple of years ago. They were sacrifices, but something went wrong, because there was never a fourth victim."

Willow swallowed. "Like when we tried to do Bethany's ritual."

"Exactly. I think the person who killed the students last time didn't know what they were doing, and the shakiness you saw in the photo were hesitation cuts."

Willow uncrossed her legs. "And now they know better, but something doesn't feel right. Why do you think there would be four sacrifices?"

"Because there were four bowls in the cavern. There's going to be another victim. We need to tell Detective Russo." I stood up, and my body was so tired, I almost collapsed back into the chair.

"Ophelia!" Willow rushed toward me and helped me sit back down. "You need to sleep."

I tried to keep my eyes open, but I begrudgingly agreed. Willow reached behind me and handed me a bottle of pills. I frowned.

"Melatonin," she explained.

"Thanks, I'll take it when I get back to my room."

"Nope." Willow grabbed my arm as I tried to stand once more. "The couch is only a few feet away. I don't trust you walking back to your dorm by yourself. You might collapse and fall down the stairs."

I didn't have the energy to argue, so I let Willow lead me to the couch. Luckily, the melatonin was the dissolvable kind, so I took one and fell into a thankfully dreamless sleep.

Willow shook me awake the next morning, and I sighed with relief. I felt more alert than I had in weeks. Sitting up, I rubbed my eyes and stretched, and when I gazed at her again, something felt wrong. Her eyes were red and puffy, like she had been crying.

"What happened?" I asked.

Willow sniffled. "Harper's dead."

My heart dropped. I didn't know Harper that well, but I knew she and Willow were close. Standing up, I wrapped Willow in my arms, and sobs wracked her body. She leaned her weight into me, and I held tighter. We stayed like that for a few minutes, and when she finally pulled away, she wiped her nose on her sleeve and took a shaky breath.

"Her hand had that damned sigil carved into it," she said, "and I would bet money that her blood now fills the fourth bowl in that old cavern."

I plopped down on the couch, and I stared at my feet.

I felt the cushion next to me sink in as Willow sat beside me.

"What in hell is going on here?" I muttered to myself.

Willow must have heard it though, because through her sniffles, she answered, "I don't know, but I know who might."

I glanced up at her. "Who?"

She pointed to my neck. My eyebrows knit together, but understanding hit me a moment later.

"No," I said, "no, no, no, no. I am *not* asking him."

Willow groaned. "You said he promised to tell you the truth to whatever you asked, right?"

"Well, yeah."

"Then ask."

I stared at Willow for several minutes, her raven black hair disheveled like she had woken up to the news of Harper's death, or run her hands through it multiple times. Her eyes were bloodshot, and she had snot dribbling from one nostril. I wasn't going to tell her because, let's face it, when you're dealing with the death of a friend, you don't tend to care how you look.

And maybe that's what made me agree to her. Because I knew what it was like to lose my best friend, and I had come to think of Willow as one of my best friends, too. She had been there for me from the beginning, just like Bethany had been. And like Bethany, I wanted to help Willow, so before I even knew what was happening, we set off down the stairs, headed straight for the headmaster's private room.

All faculty lived on campus, and even though the headmaster had his own mansion, he still had a room off a private hallway that he used during the school year. Willow was limping halfway down the corridor, and I cursed myself for not thinking about bringing her chair. She noticed my constant glances and smiled.

"I'm okay," she said, although it came out sounding more pained than she probably meant it to.

Without a word, I placed her arm over my shoulder and carried most of her weight as we made our way toward the worn wood that led to Dhazor's room.

The door creaked open and Dhazor's form emerged, his face scrunched in confusion.

"Ophelia, Miss Sasagawa. Why are you two bothering me down here?"

I clenched my jaw as I tried to keep the disdain off my face. It apparently wasn't successful. Dhazor clicked his tongue and held out his hand toward me.

I glanced between his hand and Willow, who gave me a grim nod. Willow unwrapped her arm from my shoulder, and I stepped into Dhazor's apartment.

I say apartment, because it was more opulent than any dorm room in the academy. It had an open-concept kitchen and living room with doors on either end that I guessed led to the bedroom and bathroom.

He led me to a deep red leather couch, and my muscles coiled tightly as I sat at one end. He sat down in a leather armchair across from me, giving me some space.

Dhazor stared at me, and I tried to hold his gaze and keep my body from trembling, but I failed, and I gazed at everything but him. The art that hung on the walls caught my attention, and I memorized every detail from the vibrant colors brushed on the bright white canvas in every direction, to the raised texture of the paint, and the loopy signature in the far corner. All the while, Dhazor's eyes burn a hole through me.

"Do you like it?" he finally asked.

I dragged my eyes away from the canvas to him, and I shrugged.

"It doesn't seem like your style, is all."

Dhazor chuckled. "I purchased it about fifty years ago from one of the members of my Order. He was a painter who loved life, and this particular piece was the first thing in this realm that made me feel... light."

He seemed to struggle with finding the right word, and "light" didn't seem like the word he really wanted.

"The first time you felt any sort of love was fifty years ago?" I asked.

He looked at me, his eyes wide. I had never seen him caught off guard before, and my description seemed to surprise him.

"Love." He tested the word. "No, I've loved before, and this was different. Speaking of" — he crossed a leg over his knee — "why are you here? It's not to beg me to let you out of our agreement, is it?"

I mimicked his posture, crossing my leg, and resting my hand on the arm of the couch. My hands still trembled slightly.

"No, but it does pertain to our agreement. You told me you would honestly answer any question I asked, and I have some questions."

Dhazor raised an eyebrow and cocked his mouth upward. "What questions would I have the answers to?"

His arrogance made any fear or reservations I might have had disappear, and the question eased off my tongue as easily as if I was asking about the weather.

"Whose sigil is carved into the hands of your three dead students?"

Dhazor's face stilled into a deadly calm. "Why would you think I'd have the answer?"

"Do you?"

His lips thinned, and he swallowed. He looked... nervous. But why?

"Yes," he said.

I uncrossed my legs and leaned forward, resting my arms on my thighs. "So let me ask again, whose sigil is it?"

Dhazor's expression contorted into anger, and his face looked every bit like the demon he was.

"Her name is Alvatha." There was so much venom in his words, it was a wonder this demon wasn't already dead. "Like me, she's a Divine Demon, and she's also the one who banished me to this realm."

The conversation I overheard a couple of months ago replayed in my mind.

"She's the 'lady' that the girl, Kora, was talking about down in the cavern."

"That wasn't a question," Dhazor stated.

I crossed my arms and rolled my eyes. "*Was* she the lady Kora was talking about in the cavern?"

Dhazor uncrossed his leg and his hands gripped the arms of his chair so tight I thought he would break them off. "Yes."

"Is Alvatha a brunette?" I didn't know what prompted the question, but as soon as it came out of my mouth, Dhazor went white, like maybe he needed an emergency sacrifice.

"How do you know what she looks like?"

"Because I think…" The woman in the mirror with pure black eyes popped into my mind, and what I had thought was my imagination, I now knew to be real. "Not think," I said, "I've seen her."

Dhazor's body sagged. I have never seen him slouch before, and seeing him look so… human, was creepier than the demon dog and the bowls of blood combined. What was even more disturbing was his tone when he spoke.

There was no venom, no hate or anger, just a man who sounded like he had accepted defeat.

"Then it's already too late. Call Miss Sasagawa in here and then explain everything you know to me."

Chapter Twenty-Six

WILLOW'S JOURNAL SPLAYED OPEN on the coffee table while Dhazor stood and stared out the large window in his living room. His hands were folded behind his back, and if it wasn't for the subtle rise and fall of his shoulders, I would've sworn he was a statue.

Willow sat in a chair by the couch, and I sat so close to her I felt her jump when Dhazor abruptly whirled toward us. He stalked to the table and snatched up the journal and began flipping through the pages wildly.

"You told me the Auspex said to stop it before nature brings new life." He thumbed through more pages. "But that isn't mentioned anywhere in here."

Willow shifted and crossed a leg over her knee. "The journal is my own findings. The Auspex spoke to Ophelia."

Dhazor lifted a brow as he stared at me. "And when was this?"

I straightened my back, ignoring the ache in my spine. "Halloween."

Embers flickered in his eyes. "And you're just now telling me about this?"

I snorted. "We haven't exactly been on friendly terms. The only reason I'm even telling you now is because we need your help."

The embers grew brighter, and Dhazor squeezed his eyes shut. When he reopened them, they were back to their original hazel hue.

"If you had told me earlier," he said behind clenched teeth, "then we *might* have been able to stop what's about to happen."

"What are you talking about?" Willow asked.

Dhazor huffed as he slammed the journal closed and sat back down.

"The Auspex said three more souls, correct? This was after Miss Woods' murder, so four souls in total. Add that to the fact it told you to stop it 'before nature brings new life,' and that would be —"

"The spring equinox on March twentieth," Willow finished, "We already figured that out. We have five more days."

"While you may think that, today is the Ides of March," Dhazor said, "a day commonly associated with misery and despair. Just ask Ceasar."

My face scrunched up. "Like Julius Ceasar?"

Dhazor sighed and drummed his fingers on the arm of the chair. "You should pay more attention in your English class. Yes, Julius Ceasar. His closest advisors stabbed him twenty-three times. The part of the story that's never told, however, is Alvatha influenced his murderers. She thrives off of chaos."

"So do you," I muttered.

Dhazor's lips thinned as he raised an eyebrow. I shrugged. If I was bound to him, then I might as well make his life miserable. He stood and took his cell phone out of his pocket. His thumb worked furiously as he typed out a message to someone and sent it.

A few minutes later, someone knocked on the door. Dhazor opened it, and Dorian stepped through. He rolled his eyes when he saw me, and my heart lurched. I knew he was still mad at me and probably hated me. Of course, I hadn't given him any reason not to, considering I was his father's property.

I wanted to gag. I hadn't taken the time to really process what agreeing to Dhazor meant for me, and honestly, I didn't want to. But I was no one's property, and I would make sure Dhazor, and anyone else who thought the same, knew it.

Bide your time, Ophelia. You will *find a way out of this.* I took a deep breath and got to my feet. Dhazor and Dorian were having a whispered conversation, and it seemed to be getting pretty heated.

I wiggled my way between them and pushed my hands on both of their chests.

"Can the family feud wait until after we deal with the current crisis?" I asked.

Dorian recoiled from my touch, and I had to turn away from both of them while I worked to make my expression neutral. Willow stood and grabbed the journal from the glass surface.

"Tear," she whispered as she brushed past me and handed the journal to Dorian.

Sure enough, a single tear betrayed me and slid down my cheek. I wiped it away quickly and shot Willow a grateful glance when I joined the three of them in conversation.

"...from what Ophelia told me about her visit, Detective Russo might have the photos we need."

Dhazor directed his gaze down at me. "You met with the detective who is trying to prosecute you for murder? Privately?"

I bit my bottom lip. I had hoped to keep that meeting a secret from Dhazor. If what Zachary told me about Dhazor killing his wife was true, the last thing I wanted was to put him in Dhazor's crosshairs. But since it was out...

"Detective Russo has a folder with pictures and newspaper clippings about the students who were murdered a couple years ago."

Both Dorian and Dhazor looked shocked at that, and I didn't dare say anything else, since that folder also held tons of clippings about Dhazor and his demonic dealings in Ashton.

Dhazor was the first to recover, smoothing his dark hair back. The first streaks of gray were peeking through. We had given him a sacrifice about a month ago now, but with all the stress of the murders putting the academy in the public's eye, it seemed he was fading faster than usual.

"It seems we'll need the detective's help." Dhazor said. "Although I don't —"

Three taps rang through the room, and Dhazor looked quizzically at Dorian.

"No one followed me."

Three more raps on the door echoed into the apartment, and Dhazor strode toward the sound. Splinters of wood exploded into the room. I felt myself being launched through the air. Pain erupted through my arms and face as I smashed through the glass coffee table. Red-stained shards crunched under me as I pushed myself off the ground. Dorian and Willow were lying a few feet away from me, and Dhazor was still standing, having shielded himself from the worst of the blast. Kora, the dark blond I saw in the catacombs threatening Dhazor, burst in, her hand shimmering with golden light as she lowered it to her side.

"Come now, Dhazie." She prowled toward him. "You should know you couldn't have prevented this. Now, be a gentleman and grab your... friends, and let's go greet your wife."

I wanted to protest, but the glass embedded in my skin made me want to scream every time I tried to move. Dhazor scooped me into his arms, and white-hot pain exploded throughout my body. I heard shuffling behind us as darkness clouded the edges of my vision. I tried to scream, but I couldn't get a sound out, and when the pain was too much for my body to handle, I blacked out.

I woke up to my body pulsing with pain and slightly blurry eyesight. My arms ached, and the rattle of chains sang through my head. As my vision slowly cleared, I took in my surroundings, and I wished I was still out.

We were in the catacombs. More specifically, we were in the ancient cavern that housed the obsidian bowls full of blood, and from the looks of the lit candles placed around the circle in the middle of the floor, we were about to witness the summoning of Alvatha.

"Ophelia," someone croaked to my right.

I turned my head and found Dorian, Willow, and even Dhazor chained to the wall next to me.

"What's going on?" I croaked.

"The acolytes." Dhazor didn't so much as glance in my direction. "They have everything they need, and they're now going to bring Alvatha here from her palace in Hell."

Shuffling sounded from outside the cavern. My body tensed and my chains clanged as several shadows appeared through the doorway. One by one, Order members stepped into the large cavern, most of them in maroon robes, but some of them wore cloaks of navy. Some members noticed the four of us hanging on the wall like ornaments, and confused chatter erupted through the space. The last one to step into the cavern was Alisa, her robe also a navy color that looked almost pitch black in the dim lighting.

She walked to the back of the cavern like she owned the place, and set four black taper candles by each of the obsidian bowls and lit each one with silent words. Once she was done, she whirled toward the Order members and raised her hands for silence.

"I know you all must have questions, and I promise to answer every one of them. However, to answer questions honestly, we must first have the truth from all of you."

"Who the hell is 'us'?" Odion asked, glancing up at our chains.

Alisa bore a cruel smile. If I hadn't already known she was a snake, I would have known it right then.

"Acolytes, would you stand beside me?"

The members who bore cloaks of navy followed Alisa's command. Rachel was one, as I could have guessed, but there was also a couple who I never really got to know. One of them was Gwen, the girl with the curly black hair who I had noticed always gave me a murderous look when she thought I wasn't paying attention.

The other one was a boy who I had never interacted with. He also had black hair, but he always had it styled where one side was covering his eyes. I hadn't noticed before, but both he and Gwen had similar facial features. I wondered if they were related.

Before I could voice any of my questions, I heard a commotion outside. Everyone turned their attention to the doorway as Kora stepped through the entryway and shoved Detective Russo into the cavern, who landed on his side, totally unresponsive. Kora dusted off her hands, as if touching Russo was beneath her.

"Now that everyone's here," she said, "let's get the party started. Aaron, I'm sure the detective here would like a place next to his friends."

The boy with the black hair standing beside Alisa strode forward and grabbed Zachary, but Odion firmly put one hand on his shoulder.

"No," Odion said.

Aaron looked at Odion with a mixture of annoyance and fear. I didn't blame him for being scared. Odion was tall for a sixteen-year-old and was muscular enough that I thought he had been using steroids. I asked him about it one time, and he didn't stop laughing for a solid hour.

Kora flicked her wrist, and Odion's fingers bent back one by one with a sickening crack. He screamed in pain, and Aaron's eyes widened. Kora gave him a hard stare, though, and Aaron dragged Zachary over to us. No one else dared to intervene. Kora clapped her hands twice, and everyone's attention turned to her.

"So I'm sure you all are wondering why you're here, but first I need to ask you all a question. Who here is a member of Dhazie's little club because they had no choice?"

A moment of hesitation, but Elijah's hand went up first, and everyone soon followed.

Kora nodded like she had expected that answer. She strolled toward us, hanging from the wall, and pinched Dhazor's chin between her fingers.

"And who here *hates* Dhazie?" Her voice sounded like she was talking to a pet.

Joel's hand slowly dropped to his side, and Kora nodded again. Dhazor jerked his head out of her grip. She clicked her tongue in disappointment as she took a few meaningful steps and stopped in front of me. I threw as much defiance as I could into my glare.

The room was getting thick and warm from so many bodies being in a space with no airflow and sweat trickled down my neck. Kora wiped the drop of sweat away with one finger, grazing Dhazor's brand as she did. I didn't jerk away like Dhazor, but I held my chin up higher and clenched my jaw.

Kora narrowed her eyes, and I noticed everyone in the room shifting with the obvious tension. Kora must have noticed too, because she smiled, showing two pointed canines.

"I knew he had claimed you," she said, "but I didn't know you had accepted. This just became even more fun."

She snapped her fingers, and my upraised arms, which were being held by the biting metal shackles, went limp as I fell to the ground. Before I could move a muscle, Kora grabbed me by the base of my hair and hauled me over to the circle carved into the floor. I struggled and screamed, tears stinging my eyes from the pain, but the more I wrestled to get free, the tighter her hold became until I heard a ripping sound as Kora tore strands of hair out of my scalp.

Order members parted as she dragged me into the middle of the carving and motioned for Gwen to help her. She bounced over, taking something from Aaron's hand on the way, and grabbed one of my arms. She roughly hauled both my arms around my back and bound my wrists with rope. The fibers cut into my skin, and I winced as she pulled it tighter.

"I think you shall be the one to bring forth Alvatha as her last sacrifice," Kora said, yanking my hair with one hand so my head tilted back, exposing my throat, as her other hand held an intricately carved knife in the air, flames glinting off the jagged blade.

"No!" Dorian screamed.

I hadn't heard him utter a single word since we had been down here, and hearing his voice now, so angry and full of panic, made me want to cry. I had hurt him so badly, and he still cared about what happened to me.

Squeezing my eyes shut, I replayed Dorian's voice in my head as I waited for death to take me.

Chapter Twenty-Seven

THE FINAL BLOW NEVER came, and as I opened one eye and then the other, I saw why.

Dorian had broken free from his shackles, and in his grasp, twin shadow blades rippled with dark energy. Kora snarled and finally let go of my hair as she rushed Dorian, hands contorted into claws.

There were yelps and murmurs coming from the bystanders as they tried to back up even further. I guessed the Order could dish out pain but was scared to be in the path of destruction. Gwen leapt toward the open arch of the cavern, trying to stop anyone from escaping, but several members, including Odion, his eyes shimmering with regret as he clutched his broken hand, made it out. One of the slower members sprinted after the others, but Gwen reached them and snatched the hood of their cloak. They halted as the clasp choked them, and without missing a beat, Gwen pulled a knife out of the side of the brown leather boot she wore and stabbed the member in the chest.

I shrieked, causing Kora a moment of distraction, and that was when Dorian lunged. I had seen him fight the demon dog, and I had witnessed several times where he hadn't seemed human, but this was different. He was faster than I had even thought possible, blurring through the air and stopping behind Kora. She whirled just as fast, a guttural growl erupting from her chest, and swiped her clawed hands against Dorian's face. I thought he dodged her attack, but the scream that erupted from him as he dropped one of his blades and clutched his left eye made my heart stop.

Blood seeped from between his fingers down onto the dry, dusty ground, leaving thick, dark puddles. Kora smiled triumphantly as she prowled toward him.

"Dhazor," I shouted, "do something!"

He looked like he wanted to. Bad. But no matter how hard Dhazor struggled against the chains, they wouldn't budge.

"I wouldn't count on Dhazie being of any use to you." Kora's voice was like gravel tumbling around in a dryer. "My mistress gave me a very potent potion that renders a Divine Demon's powers useless. Even skin contact, say through the almost undetectable layer sprinkled on the metal of the cuffs, is enough to fully incapacitate them."

Dhazor's face twisted into a sneer, but there were no flames in his eyes. Nothing to suggest that he had the tiniest spark of power.

Struggling to my feet, I had taken a couple of unsteady steps when Gwen blocked my path. I saw the flash of the already blood-soaked knife a second before white-hot pain shot through the left side of my abdomen. I shrieked, and the sound that blasted from my lungs was as inhuman as any demon's. My vision blurred, and I barely saw Gwen smirk before kicking me back into the middle of the circle.

Kora stepped up to the bowls, apparently satisfied that Dorian wouldn't be much more of a problem. She was probably right, too, given Dorian was now on the ground, his entire face and hand completely covered in blood. His breath was shallow, and I knew if he didn't get medical help soon, he wouldn't make it.

Of course, I was in the same boat. My hands were still bound, so I couldn't stop the warm liquid that flowed out of my body. My head felt like it was floating, and my heart raced, although I couldn't tell if that was from the blood loss or just the fear that seeped through my bones.

I heard a bubbling noise, and I concentrated on Kora. She had cut her palm, and the blood that dripped from her wound landed in the obsidian bowl on the far right. That was the bubbling I heard. The bowl of blood was boiling. She did the same thing with the other three bowls, and each one boiled after mixing with Kora's blood.

The flames surrounding me whooshed upward, making the entire cavern so bright I had to squint to see anything. The heat from the fire made my face burn. Gwen stood over me, smiling triumphantly, just out of the flame's range. The light made her look sinister, and a movement behind her caught my eye as Zachary stirred. He hadn't been bound like Kora had commanded, because glancing up at the wall, there were no more chains *to* bind him with. My breathing became labored. I couldn't think, but I had to find some way to get Zachary out of harm's way.

A thought came to me a little too late, as the ground underneath me trembled. The candles flickered and roared higher, licking the ceiling. I saw Zachary clutch his head as he tried to sit up. I wanted to call out to him to run, but no sound came out.

Gwen strode to Kora's side, and they clasped hands and chanted with their heads leaned back. I couldn't hear what they were saying, but I knew it wasn't good. The circle carved around me glowed, and I gasped as I felt a pressure on my shoulder.

Dorian had crawled his way to me, and I could tell he was also struggling to stay conscious, but he grasped my upper arm with one hand, and put pressure on my wound with the other. Together, we hobbled out of the glowing circle, and as soon as we did, the rumbling cavern stilled.

Kora and Gwen looked confused at the stillness until they saw Dorian on the ground with me, untying my restraints. Kora roared with anger and had taken only one step toward us when the cavern shook violently once more, knocking all of us to the ground.

The flames went out like a switch, dowsing us in complete darkness, and the cavern went still. Too still. I heard shuffling, and my body went rigid. Kora was going to kill us in the dark, and we wouldn't have a clue.

"Ophelia?" Zachary's whispered voice was hoarse, and also right beside me.

I sighed with relief. It wasn't Kora I had heard.

"Yeah," I panted, "it's me. Are you okay?"

"To be determined. You?"

"I-I'm hurt pretty bad."

"Can you two shut up?" Dorian growled.

He was trying to be quiet as well, but his voice carried. I heard a grunt across the room as someone moved.

Chains clinked behind us, and I wondered if Dhazor and Willow were trying to take advantage of the dark and get free.

"Oh, shit," Dhazor said.

Kora laughed in the distance, and I clutched Dorian. His body was so tense it felt like stone, and I noticed why. The cavern was flickering with light once more, washing the space with hues of orange and red. I gasped as I saw the damage to Dorian's face clearly. His eye was swollen shut, and a large gash ran diagonally from his eyebrow through the corner of his mouth down to his jawline. He didn't pay me any attention, and I noticed Kora wasn't laughing anymore either. She and Gwen were kneeling with their heads bowed. I looked a little further and gasped again.

The ring of candles flickered normally once again, and in the space I had just been bound in was a ghastly pale woman. She wore no clothes and was on her hands and knees, her long brunette hair flowing in front of her. Her hair covered most of her face, but one pure black eye stared at me through the wild strands. The ritual had been a success.

Alvatha was in the human realm.

Chapter Twenty-Eight

No one dared move. Alvatha cocked her head to the side, her hair moving with her, covering the eye that had been staring directly into my soul. She cocked her head to the other side, sniffing, her hair falling back slightly, revealing skin so smooth it looked like it had been carved out of marble. Every motion she made was quick and beast-like, and when the echo of a pebble scooting across the ground sounded just outside the cavern entrance, her movements became even more beastly.

Alvatha turned toward the sound immediately, and I heard a small gasp as she sprinted, leg over arm, toward the person peering into the cavern. My vision was turning dark as blood continued seeping from the hole in my side, but I glimpsed salon-styled brunette hair and spray-tanned skin before a guttural shriek. I shrank into Dorian's form, and Zachary gagged as sounds of tearing flesh and crunching bone carried through the space.

A sharp pain ran through me, making me jump. Dorian had pressed a finger into my wound.

"You passed out for a second," he said. "You need to stay awake." His voice was weak, and I could tell he was struggling to keep himself conscious.

"I'm sorry," I said. "For everything."

"Let's get out of here alive, then you can apologize."

Noticing Zachary wasn't next to me anymore, I tried to ask Dorian where he was, but he shushed me.

Alvatha gracefully sauntered back into the cavern on two legs. Blood and sinew coated her skin from her mouth down to her chest. More blood and bits of gore also coated her slender fingers. She stopped in front of Kora and Gwen, who hadn't moved from their kneeling position. She stared down at them and licked her fingers one by one.

"My faithful servant," she said, her voice like honey coated barbed wire, "and one of my four — I guess now it's three — acolytes. You both may stand."

Kora and Gwen did as commanded. Kora had nothing but pride and adoration on her face, but tears were silently falling down Gwen's cheeks.

Alvatha clicked her tongue and ran a finger down Gwen's face, wiping away a tear and leaving a streak of blood in its place.

"Don't cry, dear," she said. "Your friend Rachel was delicious."

A loud clank behind me made me jump. Alvatha whirled to find Zachary working to shake loose the second bolt of the shackles holding Dhazor from the wall. Zachary didn't even pause, he just kept wiggling the chains back and forth. Small bits of stone crumbled to the ground as the bolt became looser, but Alvatha was fast.

Willow wiggled her body wildly and yanked on her own chains, trying to free herself, but it wasn't working nearly as well. I had to do something, but I could barely move. Dorian was in the same situation, judging by the weak hold he had on me.

I glanced toward Kora, who was just standing outside the ring of candles, her arms crossed, waiting for her mistress to finish us off. The candles were still lit, the liquid wax pooling around the flame, and I had a wild idea. Without warning, I pushed away from Dorian. He tried to grab me, but with one eye out of commission, his depth perception wasn't the greatest, and the only thing he grabbed was air.

Kora noticed my movement, slow as it was, and snarled. My breathing became labored and my knees wobbled. Gwen was still mourning Rachel (I wasn't), and with Alvatha no longer in front of her, she had sunk to her knees and was sobbing into her hands. My body gave out just as I reached the outer ring, and Kora lunged. My teeth clenched and my vision went black around the edges as I stretched out my arm. Pain pulled at the still-gaping wound, but I wrapped my fingers around the warm, squishy wax of the candle, and smashed it into Kora's face. She screamed in agony, pulling back.

Alvatha screamed as if she had been the one who had melted wax all over her face. My vision was going in and out, and my body felt weightless.

Which it kind of was.

Alvatha had grabbed me by the throat and lifted me in the air, my legs dangling like a rag doll. I willed my legs to move, to kick her anywhere I could reach, but the most I managed to do was twitch my leg muscles. Alvatha laughed and squeezed my neck. I grunted softly as I started to black out.

"Stop. Please."

Alvatha relaxed her grip, and for a moment I thought I had been the one to speak, but she turned her head to the side. I followed her gaze, my head moving in slow motion, and Dhazor was on the ground, kneeling by Dorian's limp body. Zachary was working on releasing Willow's chains from the wall, but Alvatha wasn't paying them any mind.

"What did you say?" she asked.

"I said... don't hurt her." His voice held no warmth or sadness. Nothing that would give away what he was feeling. "I'll do whatever you wish, but let her go."

Alvatha chuckled darkly. I felt my body flying, and a hard crack of pain as everything finally went black.

An annoying beeping woke me, and I cracked my eyelids open a fraction to bright white light searing my pupils. I quickly squeezed my eyes shut again and groaned. I was dead. There was no way I had survived Alvatha.

The beeping increased, and I heard a soft chuckle to my left. I turned my head toward the sound, but didn't open my eyes.

"It's okay, Bubbles. You're safe."

Dorian? Was he dead, too?

I popped one eye open and found him sitting in a chair upholstered in a muted shade of purple vinyl. He had gauze wrapped around one side of his face, completely covering his left eye. The back of his dark brown hair was sticking straight up like he had been lying down for a while, and he was wearing a dress. No, not a dress. A gown. A hospital gown. He wasn't dead, and that meant neither was I.

My other eye opened as I fully took in my surroundings. Light beige walls surrounded me. The color looked abnormal against the white linoleum floor, and the beeping shrieked once again as I looked to my other side. The sound was coming from the monitor, tracking my vital signs.

I tried to sit up and sucked in a sharp breath. My abdomen was on fire. Dorian shot up from his chair and helped me into a comfortable position. I tried to smile, but it came out as a wince. He smoothed down my hair, his fingers snagging some tangles.

"Be careful," he said, "your body took a beating."

"So did yours." My voice was so hoarse I could barely speak.

I cleared my throat and tried to talk again, but that only made it worse. Dorian fumbled for the styrofoam cup on the table at the foot of the bed. It took a few tries, but he grabbed it and handed it to me. I took a sip of the ice water, reveling in the sensation.

"What happened to everyone?" I asked.

Dorian sat back down and sighed. "Rachel is dead, as you know. So is one other member. Everyone else made it out alive, miraculously. The Order has basically been dismantled, between people being fed up with serving my dad and Alvatha's acolytes being on the run. My dad and Alvatha have disappeared. I don't know where they went, but I'm sure they'll rear their despicable heads at some point."

"What about Willow?"

Dorian's lips curled up slightly. "She's fine. Actually, I'm pretty sure she was the only one of us who escaped relatively unscathed. Russo has a couple of broken bones, and Gwen had a complete breakdown and is being treated in the psychiatric unit. I tried talking to her when you were still out, but she's not speaking. And me" — he gestured to his face — "my eye is gone, and I'll have a gnarly scar."

I reached out and traced around the bandage, being careful not to touch the surface of the gauze. Dorian shut his eye and exhaled. When he opened it again, he looked down at his hands.

"This doesn't change anything, you know," he said.

"Doesn't change what?"

Dorian looked at me and tried to raise an eyebrow, but the bandage prevented him. He gestured to my neck. I grazed my skin and, sure enough, the raised edge of Dhazor's sigil was still branded on the side of my throat.

I pursed my lips. "You should know it doesn't mean anything. You even said yourself he was gone. Why — why can't that be enough?"

Dorian barked out a humorless laugh. "Don't think he's forgotten about you. He'll come back, and once he does, you're his. Even if he doesn't..."

He trailed off and bit his lip. I scooted myself up on the hard mattress, positioning myself to look at him better. Dorian shook his head.

"Even if Dhazor doesn't come back to claim you, I can't trust you anymore. You did that" — he pointed to the brand — "without even talking to me about it. I thought we were on the same page, and you betrayed me. I-I can't be with someone who does that."

Tears stung my eyes, and I blinked them back.

"But I love you," I said. It was a weak excuse, and we both knew it.

"Love isn't enough."

I wanted to say more. I needed to explain to him I had no choice. He knew Dhazor was threatening my mom, but he didn't understand how little Dhazor cared if she died. The door to the room opened, and a nurse walked in, her high copper-colored ponytail swishing with every movement.

"It's time for pain meds," she said. "You ready for them now?"

"She is," Dorian said. "Her stitches have been hurting."

Stitches? The nurse nodded and pushed the plunger of a syringe into the bag of fluids that was hanging from the monitor. She waited for a minute, and when my eyelids drooped, she smiled down at me and left. Dorian stood up from his chair and moved to follow the nurse out. My fingers snatched the corner of his gown, and he halted.

"Ophelia" — his voice cracked — "Don't make this harder than it has to be."

The meds were dragging me under, but I had to get him to see how much I loved him and how sorry I was. I tried to get those very words out, but I'm pretty sure it came out as gibberish. He leaned down and kissed the top of my head, lingering longer than was really necessary.

"Be happy and stay safe," he whispered into my hair as the meds kicked in and dragged me to sleep.

Chapter Twenty-Nine

I T WAS A FULL week before I could go back to school, and even then I had to take it easy. The seven stitches it had taken to seal the knife wound had been taken out the day of my discharge, so I didn't need to worry about that, but the two fractured ribs were still an issue, as was the iron deficiency from all the blood loss. Detective Russo had called Mom as soon as he was able, and she flew into Ashton the next day. Apparently, Dhazor had kept his promise when we made the deal and flew Mom back home, unharmed. She told me the hospital had to give me two transfusions to replace the blood, and that if I had gotten treatment even a moment later, I would have died.

Mom was also staying in Ashton until the end of the school year. She seemed more relaxed being in town since Dhazor disappeared, and kept apologizing over and over, telling me she never meant for me to get into any of this, and she wished she had known.

I hadn't confronted her about the picture Zachary had shown me, and I didn't know if I was ever going to. She had been a member of the Order, but either she didn't remember, or she was fantastic at hiding that fact. Mom also seemed to have forgotten about what happened to her at Dhazor's mansion, and even though I had thousands of burning questions, I didn't want to make her remember such a horrific night. She seemed to know what the sigil on my neck meant, though, because whenever she thought I wasn't paying attention, she would stare at it with a mixture of concern and fear. Whether that indicated her knowledge of Dhazor, or just her intuition telling her something was off, I didn't know.

One morning, at seven-thirty sharp, I heard two knocks at the door to the common room. I rolled my eyes as I answered it, and Willow rolled in, asking me if I was ready. Willow had escorted me to every class since I returned, and since she was using her chair, I rode the service elevator with her. I didn't know why she was using her chair so much now, but Dorian was right. She hadn't suffered any other injuries other than a dislocated wrist and some dark bruising where the chains held her.

We made our way to the auditorium where school officials had organized a "special assembly." Willow and I had speculated the assembly was about the headmaster suddenly going missing, and we were right. We took our seats, and the assistant principal, Mr. Wells, called the student body to attention via screeching feedback from the mic.

"Yes, yes, settle down. As you all know, our esteemed headmaster has taken a rather... unexpected vacation, so until further notice, I will take over for the last few weeks of the school year as interim headmaster until we can find a more permanent addition. Furthermore, I have heard all of your complaints about your friends leaving suddenly in the middle of the night, and rest assured, we have worked very closely with the Ashton police department. They have concluded that this was a group that planned to run away together and executed that plan."

It was true. When I came back to my dorm after getting discharged, Alisa had hastily cleared out her room. I didn't know where she and the other members of the Order had run off to, but I hoped they were at least safe. Well, I hoped the Order members were safe. Alvatha's acolytes were another matter. I couldn't fathom why Alisa would want to worship such a... demon, but maybe, like the currency members, she had no say in the matter.

The assembly concluded, and while everyone was filing out, I noticed Zachary standing at the very back of the auditorium. We locked eyes, and he motioned for me to follow him. Walking toward him, I dodged students as they stopped in the middle of the aisle to talk. I was dodging one such student when I bumped into another. I winced, my stab wound still tender, and noticed I had run into the one person who made me hurt worse than my still-healing gash.

Dorian.

Even with the dark sunglasses he wore, and the thick, scabbed laceration running down the length of his face, I still knew it was him. I couldn't see his expression through the glasses, but his lips were set in a thin line. We looked at each other for what felt like an eternity. I opened my mouth to say something, anything, but he turned and walked away from me before I could.

I sighed and trudged the rest of the way to where Zachary stood.

"We need to talk. Privately," he said.

I followed him to the office and several students stared and whispered. I tried to ignore them, but a detective was still escorting a murder suspect awaiting trial to a private area. The rumor mill would be abuzz.

Once the door to Dhazor's — or I guess now Mr. Wells' office — was shut, Zachary sighed.

"Sorry for that. I know none of this has been easy on you."

I shrugged as I sat down in one of the two chairs that sat in front of the desk. "I'm used to it. Besides, people whispering about me is probably the tamest thing I've encountered here."

"I know. Speaking of..."

Zachary dropped the manila folder he had been carrying on the desk between us as he sat in the high-backed executive chair. He opened the folder to a single piece of paper with a lot of squiggly lines.

I grabbed the paper and stared at it before turning it sideways and upside down, trying to figure out what the lines meant. I was at a loss.

"What is this?" I asked.

Zachary smirked. "That is proof you're innocent in all four of the killings."

The thin piece of mashed-up trees now seemed like a priceless artifact that belonged in a museum.

"Are you serious?"

He nodded. A smile spread across my face.

"The DA is dropping all charges. You're free."

My face fell as I absentmindedly ran a finger down my neck. "Yeah."

"Ophelia, there's something else." Zachary bit his full lip and fidgeted with his hands.

I set the paper down and crossed my arms, waiting for him to speak. He swallowed and spoke.

"Those are the results I've been waiting for. I got them the day... everything happened and was coming to tell you about it when I was cornered by that buzz-cut blond b—"

He closed his eyes and took a deep breath. And another.

"Bitch?" I finished for him.

He chuckled, despite biting his lip to keep from laughing. He opened his eyes, composed himself once more, and continued.

"Anyway, the results prove your innocence, but also someone else's guilt."

I furrowed my brow and shifted in my seat. "Whose?"

"Alisa's. She killed Bethany Woods, and Ernest Elrod, and Jacob, and Harper. The lab and the coroner confirmed it. The knife also matches the carvings from the murders a couple of years ago, so it looks like Alisa is good for those as well."

My arms fell to my side. I didn't want to believe it, but the more I thought about it, the more the pieces clicked together.

She lived in the room next to Bethany, so of course, she had the opportunity to kill her. Framing me was just as easy for the same reason. She hated Harper, so killing her would have been a bonus, and Ernest could speak to the demonic realm, so he had to go in case he revealed Alvatha's plans. But why kill Jacob? As far as I could tell, he was innocent in all this.

"Ophelia?"

I blinked several times, bring myself back to the present.

"Sorry," I muttered.

"It's okay." Zachary stood up, tucked the folder containing the evidence against Alisa under his arm, and headed for the door.

I followed but stopped as he hesitated with his hand on the handle.

"I'm leaving Ashton," he said. "I think you should too. Go home, find another school, and be normal."

"I'll think about it."

He didn't seem too satisfied with that answer, but didn't pursue it any further as he opened the door and left.

I stood in the open doorway and grazed the side of my neck once more. Maybe he was right. Mom and I could leave. We could go home, or move somewhere else entirely and start fresh, but as I looked back on everything I had endured over the course of this school year, I knew it wouldn't have been right. It wouldn't have been me. Maybe it would have been when all this started, but I didn't recognize that girl anymore. Alisa had to answer for her crimes, Alvatha and Dhazor were still out there causing who knew how much trouble, and I still had to break the agreement with Dhazor, and fix things with Dorian. No, I wasn't going to run. I was going to fight.

And I was going to win.

About the Author

Julie Caldwell was born and raised in Oklahoma where she still resides with her little black cats, Absynthe and Hemlock. Julie fell in love with reading when she was very little when her mother would read stories to her at bedtime.

Her love of reading quickly translated into her love of writing, first with poems, and then with full length novels. She has a love of anything mythological or having to do with the occult. Her hobbies include playing video games, and photography.

She is a 2024 recipient of the NextGen Under 30 Oklahoma Award, which honors creative and innovative leaders Under 30 years old in Oklahoma, and in 2025 her Of Witches and Ruin Duology was featured as two of Oklahoma's bestsellers.

Acknowledgements

This book would not have been possible without so many people behind the scenes helping me to make it happen.

First, I would like to acknowledge my best friend, Cal. From cheering me on when life got hard and deadlines loomed, to kicking my ass in gear with "productivity nights", they have been there for me through thick and thin, and I could not ask for a better bestie. I love you, Cal.

Second, I want to thank Cal's family who welcomed me with open arms and have been gracious and loving toward me since day one. They are the definition of love, and I couldn't find kinder people if I tried.

I would also like to thank my therapist for helping me realize that I am more than my trauma, and I can do anything I set my mind to, while also giving me the occasional reality check, and making me a better person.

Next, I would like to thank my wonderful friend Lauren. We met under unusual circumstances, but I can't think of another person who is more generous and hardworking. Even with everything she does (and she does a lot!), she still has time to help me organize book signings, or when I can't figure out how to write a business email.

And I can't leave out my wonderful editor, Emily, who has helped me become a better writer and helped make this book as amazing as it is.

Lastly, I want to thank my author and reader community on social media. I am so grateful to be a part of such a wonderful and supportive community.

Secret
of the
Acolytes

Official Spotify Playlist

Scan With Your Spotify App

Don't Forget to Rate and Review!